ACCLAIM FOR J.R. RAIN

"Be prepared to lose sleep!"
—**James Rollins**, international bestselling author of *The Doomsday Key*, on J.R. Rain's *The Lost Ark*

"I love this!"
—**Piers Anthony**, bestselling author of *Xanth*, on J.R. Rain's *Moon Dance*

"*Dark Horse* is the best book I've read in a long time!"
—**Gemma Halliday**, RITA Award–winning author of *Spying in High Heels*

"*Moon Dance* is absolutely brilliant!"
—**Lisa Tenzin-Dolma**, author of *Understanding the Planetary Myths*

"Powerful stuff!"
—**Aiden James**, author of *Deadly Night*, on J.R. Rain's *Arthur*

"*Moon Dance* is a must-read. If you like Janet Evanovich's Stephanie Plum, bounty hunter, be prepared to love J.R. Rain's Samantha Moon, vampire private investigator."
—**Eve Paludan**, author of *Letters from David*

"Impossible to put down. J.R. Rain's *Moon Dance* is a fabulous urban fantasy replete with multifarious and unusual characters, a perfectly synchronized plot, vibrant dialogue, and sterling witticism, all wrapped in a voice that is as beautiful as it is rich and vividly intense as it is relaxed."
—**April Vine**, author of *The Midnight Rose*

THE BODY DEPARTED

OTHER BOOKS BY J.R. RAIN

The Lost Ark
Elvis Has Not Left the Building
Cursed! (with Scott Nicholson)
The Vampire Club (with Scott Nicholson)
Silent Echo (coming soon)

VAMPIRE FOR HIRE SERIES
Moon Dance
Vampire Moon
American Vampire
Moon Child
Christmas Moon
Vampire Dawn
Vampire Games
Moon Island (coming soon)

SAMANTHA MOON SHORT STORIES
Teeth
Vampire Nights
Vampire Blues
Vampire Dreams
Halloween Moon

JIM KNIGHTHORSE TRILOGY
Dark Horse
The Mummy Case
Hail Mary

SPINOZA TRILOGY
The Vampire with the Dragon Tattoo
The Vampire Who Played Dead
The Vampire in the Iron Mask

THE BODY DEPARTED

J.R. RAIN

THOMAS & MERCER

Published by Thomas & Mercer
PO Box 400818
Las Vegas, NV 89140

ISBN-13: 9781611099386
ISBN-10: 1611099382
Library of Congress Control Number: 2012920544

Was it doubted that those who corrupt their
own bodies conceal themselves;
And if those who defile the living are as bad
as they who defile the dead?
And if the body does not do as much as the Soul?
And if the body were not the Soul, what is the Soul?

—"I Sing the Body Electric"
Leaves of Grass, Walt Whitman

1

I stepped through the wall and into my daughter's bedroom.

She was sleeping contentedly on her side. It was before dawn, and the building was quiet. The curtains were open, and the sky beyond was black. If there were any stars, they were lost to the LA smog. The curtains were covered with ponies, as was most of the room. A plastic pony light switch, a pony bed lamp, pony wallpaper and bedspread. Someday she would outgrow her obsession with ponies, although I secretly hoped not.

A girl and her pony, it's a beautiful thing.

I stepped closer to my sleeping daughter, and as I did so, she shifted slightly toward me. She mewed like a newborn kitten. Crimson light from her alarm clock splashed over her delicate features, highlighting a slightly upturned nose and impossibly big eyes. Sometimes, when she slept, her closed eyelids fluttered and danced. But not tonight. Tonight she was sleeping deeply, no doubt dreaming of sugar and spice and everything nice.

Or of Barbies and boys and everything in between.

I wondered if she ever dreamed of me. I'm sure she did at times. Were those dreams good or bad? Did she ever wake up sad and missing her father?

Do you want *her to wake up sad?*

No, I thought. *I want her to wake up rested, restored, and full of peace.*

I stepped away from the far wall and glided over to the small chair in the corner of her room. We had made the chair together one weekend, a father-daughter project for the Girl Scouts. To her credit, she did most of the work.

I sat in it now, lowering my weightless body into it, mimicking the act of sitting. Unsurprisingly, the chair didn't creak.

As I sat, my daughter rolled over in her sleep, facing me. Her aura, usually blue and streaked with red flames, often reacted to my presence, as it did now. The red flames crackled and gravitated toward me like a pulsating static ball, sensing me like I sensed it.

As I continued to sit, the lapping red flames grew in intensity, snapping and licking the air like solar flares on the surface of the sun. My daughter's aura always reacted this way to me. But only in sleep. Somehow her subconscious recognized me, or perhaps it was her soul. Or both. Either way, from this subconscious state, she would sometimes speak to me, as she did now.

"Hi, Daddy."

"Hi, baby," I said.

"Mommy said you got hurt real bad."

"Yes, I did."

"Mommy said that a bad man hurt you and you got killed."

"Mommy's right, but I don't want you thinking about that right now, okay?"

"Okay," she said sleepily. "Am I dreaming, Daddy?"

"Yes, baby."

We were quiet and she shifted subtly, lifting her face toward me, her eyes still closed in sleep. There was a sound from outside her window, a light tapping. I ignored it, but it came again and again, and then with more consistency. I looked over my shoulder and saw that it was raining. I looked back at my daughter and thought of the rain, remembering how it felt on my skin, on my face. Or, rather, I was *trying* to remember. Lately, such memories of the flesh were getting harder and harder to recall.

"It's raining, Daddy," she said.

"Yes."

"Do you live in the rain?"

"No."

"Where do you live, Daddy?"

"I live here, with you."

"But you're dead."

I said nothing. I hated to be reminded of this, even by my daughter.

"Why don't you go to heaven, Daddy?"

I thought about that. I think about that a lot, actually. I said, "Daddy still has work to do."

"What kind of work?"

"Good work."

"I miss you," she said. "I miss you so much. I think about you every day. I'm always crying. People at school say I'm a crybaby."

"You're not a crybaby," I said. "You're just sad." My heart broke all over again. "It's time to go back to sleep, angel."

"Okay, Daddy."

"I love you, sweetie."

"I love you, too, Daddy."

I drifted up from the small wooden chair and moved across the room the way I do—silently and easily—and at the far wall, I looked back at her. Her aura had subsided, although some of it still flared here and there. For her to relax—truly relax—I needed to leave her room entirely.

And so I did. Through the wall.

To hell with doors.

2

I was standing behind him, reading the newspaper from over his shoulder, as I did every morning.

His name was Jerrold, and he was close to sixty and close to retirement. He lived alone and seemed mostly happy. He was addicted to Internet poker, but as far as I could tell, that was his only vice.

Thank God.

He turned the paper casually, snapping it taut, then reached for his steaming mug of coffee, heavy with sugar and cream, and took a long sip. I could smell the coffee—or at least a *hint* of it, just like I could smell a hint of his aftershave and hair gel. My senses were weak at best.

As he set down the mug, some of the coffee sloshed over the rim and onto the back of his hand. He yelped and shook his hand. I could see that it had immediately reddened.

Pain.

I hadn't known pain in quite a long time. My last memory of it was when I had been working at a friend's house, cutting carpet, and nearly severed my arm off.

I looked down at my translucent arm now. Although nearly imperceptible, the scar was still there—or at least the ghostly hint of it.

Still cursing under his breath, Jerrold turned back to his paper. So did I. He scanned the major headlines, and I scanned them along with him. After all, he was my hands in this situation.

He read through some local Los Angeles news, mostly political stuff that would have bored me to tears had I tears to be bored with. I glanced over at his coffee while he read, trying to remember what it tasted like. I think I remembered.

I think.

Hot, roasted, bitter, and sweet. I knew the words, but I was having a hard time recalling the actual flavor. That scared me.

Jerrold turned the page. As he did so, something immediately caught my eye; luckily, it caught his eye, too.

A piano teacher had been murdered at St. Luke's, a converted monastery that was now being used as a Catholic church and school. Lucy Randolph was eighty-six years old and just three days shy of celebrating her sixtieth anniversary with her husband.

I had known Mrs. Randolph. In fact, she had been my own music teacher back when I was a student at St. Luke's. She had been kind to a fault, a source of inspiration and joy to her students, and especially to me.

And now, according to the report, someone had strangled her, leaving her for dead on the very piano she had taught on. Perhaps the very same piano *I* had been taught on.

Damn.

Jerrold clucked his tongue and shook his head and moved on to the next page, but I had seen enough. I stepped away.

"You're still young, Jerrold," I said to him. "Lose fifteen pounds and find someone special—and ditch the gambling."

As I spoke, the small hairs on the back of his neck stood up and his aura shifted toward me. He shivered unconsciously and turned the page.

3

We were in Pauline's apartment.

She was drinking an apple martini and I wasn't, which was a damn shame. At the moment, I was sitting in an old wingback chair, and she was on the couch, one bare foot up on a hand-painted coffee table that could have doubled as a modern piece of abstract art.

"If you ever need any extra money," I said, "you could always sell your coffee table on eBay."

"It's not for sale," she said. "Ever."

"What if you were homeless and living on the streets and needed money?"

"Then I would be homeless and living on the streets with the world's most bitchin' hand-painted coffee table."

Her name was Pauline, and she was my best—and only—friend. She was also a world-famous medium. She could hear me, see me, and sometimes even touch me. Hell, she could even read my thoughts, which was a bit disconcerting for me. She was a full-figured woman, with perhaps the most beautiful face I had ever seen. She often wore her long brown hair haphazardly, a look that would surely have your average California girl running back to the bathroom mirror. Pauline was not your average California girl. She wasn't your average girl by any definition, spending as much of her time in the world of the dead as in the world of the living. Luckily, she just so happened to live in the very building I was presently haunting.

"Yeah, lucky me," said Pauline, picking up on my thoughts.

She did her readings out of a small office near downtown Los Angeles, usually working with just one or two clients a day. Some of her sessions lasted longer than others, and tonight she was home later than usual, hitting the booze hard, as she often did. I wouldn't call her a drunk, but she was damn close to being one.

"I'm not a drunk," Pauline said absently, reading my thoughts again. "I can stop anytime I want. The booze just helps me... release."

"Release?" I asked.

"Yeah, to forget. To unwind. To *un*-everything."

"You should probably not drink so much," I said.

She regarded me over her martini glass. Her eyes were bloodshot. Her face gleamed with a fine film of sweat. She wasn't as attractive when she was drunk.

"Thanks," she said sarcastically. "And do you even remember what it's like being drunk?"

I thought about that. "A little. And that was below the belt."

"Do you even have a belt?"

I looked down at my slightly glowing, ethereal body. Hell, even my clothing glowed. It was the same clothing I had been wearing on the night I was murdered two years ago: a white T-shirt and long red basketball shorts, my usual sleeping garb. I was barefoot, and I suspected my hair was a mess, since I had been shot to death in my sleep. Dotting my body were the various bloody holes where the bullets had long ago entered my living flesh.

"No belt," I said. "Then again, no shoes, either."

She laughed, which caused some of her martini to slosh over the rim. She cursed and licked her fingers like a true alcoholic.

"Oh, shut up," she said.

"Waste not, want not," I said.

She glared at me some more as she took a long pull on her drink. When she set it down, she missed the center of the cork coaster by about three inches. Now part of the glass sat askew on the edge of the coaster, and the whole thing looked like it might tip over. She didn't notice or care.

Pauline worked with spirits all day. Early on, she had tried her best to ignore my presence. But I knew she could see me, so I pursued her relentlessly until she finally acknowledged my existence.

"And now I can't get rid of you," she said.

"You love me," I said. "Admit it."

"Yeah," she said, "I do. Call me an idiot, but I do."

"Idiot," I said. "Besides, I'm different than those other ghosts."

"Yeah? How so?"

"I'm a ghost on a mission."

"Could that sound more corny?" she said.

"Maybe after a few more drinks," I said.

"So how's the mission coming along?" she asked. We had been over this before, perhaps dozens of times.

"I don't know," I said. "It's not like I'm getting a lot of feedback from anyone—or anything."

"And when will you be done with your mission?" she asked.

"I don't know that, either."

"And what, exactly, is your mission?" As she spoke, she peered into the empty glass with one eye.

"To save my soul."

"Oh, yeah, that. And you're sure it's not too late to save your soul? I mean, you are dead, after all."

8

"It's never too late," I said.

"And you know that, how?" she asked.

"Because I'm not in hell yet."

"You're haunting an old apartment building in Los Angeles," she said. "Sounds a bit like hell to me."

"But I can see my wife and daughter whenever I want," I countered. "Can't be that bad."

"Your wife has already remarried," said Pauline. "And weren't you two separated at the time of your death?"

We had been, but the details of our separation were lost to me. We had financial problems, I seemed to recall, which had led to many arguments. What we had argued about was anyone's guess. But the arguments had been heated and impassioned, and in the end, I had moved out—but not very far. To stay close to my daughter, I had rented an apartment in the same building.

"Yes, we had been separated," I said. "And thank you for reminding me of that."

"Just keeping it real," said Pauline indifferently. "Besides, there is no hell."

"How do you know?"

"I talk to the dead, remember? And not just ghosts," she added, "but those who have passed on."

"Passed on to heaven?" I asked.

"Passed on to *something*," she said. "Neither heaven nor hell. A spirit world—and it's waiting for you."

I didn't believe that. I believed in heaven and hell, and I was certain, as of this moment, that I was going to hell. "Well, it can keep on waiting. I'm not ready to pass on."

"Obviously."

"I need to work some things out," I said.

"And then what?" she asked.

"And then I will accept my fate."

She nodded. "But for now, you hope to change your fate."

"Yes."

She looked at me with bloodshot eyes. Sitting on the couch, she had tucked her bare feet under her. Now her painted-red toes peeked out like frightened little mice.

"Nice imagery," she said, wiggling her toes. "So you still can't remember why you are going to hell?"

"No," I said.

"But it was something bad."

"Very bad," I said.

"Bad enough to burn forever?" she asked.

"Somebody died, I think."

"So you've said, but you still don't remember who or why."

I shook my head. "No, but it happened a long, long time ago."

"And with your death," she added, "it was the first of your memories to disappear."

She was right. My memories were disappearing at an alarming rate. The earlier memories of my life were mostly long gone. "Yeah, something like that," I said.

"And now you're afraid to pass on because you think you are going to hell, even though you can't remember *why* you are going to hell."

"It's a hell of a conundrum," I said.

She nodded, then got up, padded into the adjoining kitchen, and poured herself another drink. When she came back and sat, some of her drink splashed over the rim of her glass.

"Don't say a word," she cautioned me.

I laughed and drifted over to the big bay window and looked out over Los Angeles, which glittered and pulsed five stories below. At this hour, Los Feliz Boulevard was a parking lot dotted with red brake lights as far as the eye could see. I had heard once that it was one of the busiest streets in the world. Standing here now, I believed it.

After a while, Pauline came over and stood next to me. Actually, some of her was standing *inside* me. She shivered with the sensation, apologized, and stepped back. Ghostly etiquette.

I thought of my sweet music teacher. According to the paper, she had been murdered just days away from her sixtieth wedding anniversary. *Sixtieth.*

Anger welled up within me. As it did so, a rare warmth spread through me. Mostly, my days were filled with bone-chilling cold, minus the bones. But whenever strong emotion was involved, such as anger, I became flush with energy. And when that happened—

"Hey," said Pauline. "Someone's making a rare appearance."

And so I was. So much so that I could actually see myself reflected in the big sliding glass door. Next to me was Pauline, looking beautiful but drunk. Bloody wounds covered my body— in particular, my forehead, neck, and chest.

I didn't get to see myself often, and despite my anger, I took advantage of this rare opportunity. Pale and ethereal, I was just a vague suggestion of what I had once been—and I was growing vaguer as the years pressed on. There was stubble on my jaw, and my dark hair was indeed askew. Eternal bedhead.

Great.

"But you're still a cutie," said Pauline, giggling, now almost entirely drunk.

And with those words and that infectious giggle, my anger abated and I started fading away again.

"Tell me about your murdered friend," said Pauline.

"She wasn't necessarily a friend."

11

She explored my mind a bit more. "My apologies. Your piano teacher from grade school."

"Yes."

"Why would someone kill her?" she asked.

"I don't know."

She paused, then nodded knowingly. "I see you intend to find out."

"Yes."

"And perhaps save your soul in the process?"

"That's the plan," I said. "For now."

"You do realize you have limits to where you can go and what you can do, right?"

I shrugged. "Minor technicalities."

4

The girl could see me, and amazingly, she wasn't afraid.

Since she and her mother were new tenants in the apartment building I haunted, I swung by to say hello like any good neighbor. And by "swinging by," I mean I walked straight through their front door and into their living room.

To my surprise, the little girl immediately looked up from where she was sitting at a desk in the far corner of the room. Her eyes impossibly huge and innocent. She was young, perhaps seven or eight, about the age of my own daughter.

Hey, maybe they'll be friends.

I was in a low-energy state, which meant I was just a murky drift of ectoplasm that was vaguely humanoid and barely visible, even to myself. It would take a keenly aware medium to see me now.

But she sees you now, I thought.

Indeed. And a thrill coursed through me.

She stood slowly from her swivel chair. I could hear her mother in the other room, unpacking and singing contentedly to herself, unaware that her daughter had just made contact with the Great Beyond.

The girl approached me carefully, as if walking a tightrope. As if, remarkably, she was afraid of scaring *me* off. Tough girl. She stopped ten feet away. There was a smudge of chocolate in the corner of her mouth. I could see her brain working behind those impossibly huge eyes.

"I'm not afraid of you," she said. "I see ghosts all the time."

I smiled and impressed the image of a friend into her mind.

"You're a good ghost," she said, nodding. "Some ghosts are not good; some are bad."

I next tried impressing the images of my daughter and wife and my apartment down the hall, but none of this got a response from her. She was attuned, but not highly attuned. Like a deaf musician.

"You don't have to talk if you don't want to," she said. "Mommy thinks I make up the ghosts, anyway. Maybe I do. Maybe ghosts are just *figmentals* of my imagination, like she says."

Despite her bravado, there was still a touch of fear in her eyes. I smiled reassuringly, but I wasn't sure if she could see the fine details of my smile. She studied me a moment longer, shrugged, then plodded back to her chair. Once seated, she swiveled around and faced me, her bare feet dangling just inches from the faux-hardwood floor.

I drifted closer and raised my finger, pointing at her computer.

She followed my finger. "The computer?"

I nodded exaggeratedly so that she could not mistake the gesture.

"What about the computer?" she asked.

I focused on the image of a writing program.

She studied me. "Do you want me to open Word?"

I nodded vigorously.

She turned back to her computer and clicked open Word for Windows. When a blank screen appeared on the monitor, I leaned across her body and drew energy from both her and the computer, and struck a key on the keyboard. Granted, my finger disappeared down *through* the key, but luckily, the sensitive keyboard recognized my touch. Ghosts and machines sort of go hand in hand.

A letter appeared on the monitor before her, a *Y*. I continued typing until I had formed a complete sentence.

Yes, I'm a ghost was my reply.

The little girl, who had scooted back in her chair to allow me room, squealed with delight, clapping. "You can type!"

Yes, I responded, the words appearing on the white screen.

"Do I need to type back?" she asked me.

No, I wrote. *I can hear you just fine. What's your name?*

She scooted back in her chair, giving me enough room to type. "Kaira," she said. "So how long have you been dead?"

Two years, I think.

"You think?" she asked.

It's getting harder and harder to remember dates.

She screwed up her little face. "I can see that, I think."

You are a smart girl, Kaira.

"So are you really a good ghost?"

Yes.

"Then why didn't you go to heaven?"

I thought about that, my fingers hovering over the keyboard. She was just a little girl—no need to burden her with too much information.

It's not time, I wrote.

"You're not going to heaven, are you?" she said. She was more sensitive than I thought.

I hesitated, then typed my reply.

No, I don't think so.

15

"You're going to hell," she said.

I think so, yes. But I'm working on that.

She pushed her chair back and stood suddenly. She looked at me warily. "Were you a bad man?"

Yes, I wrote. *I'm sure I was. But I don't remember what I did.*

"But you said you are a good ghost."

I'm a good ghost, but I was a bad man.

She continued watching me cautiously. I didn't blame her. "What did you mean when you said you were 'working on that'?"

I typed, *Means, I'm trying to be a better person.*

"But it's too late," she said. "You're already dead."

A minor technicality.

"What's a technicality?"

Means I'm working on it, I typed, then added a winky face, complete with semicolon and parentheses.

"Kaira, honey," called her mother from the next room, "who are you talking to out there?"

"No one, Mommy," said the little girl.

"Come and help me, sweetie."

"Okay, Mommy." She quickly closed the Word document and turned to me. "I got to go," she whispered. "You seem like a good ghost. I hope you don't go to hell."

"That makes two of us," I said, but she showed no indication of hearing me. I smiled at her again and exited the same way I had come, through the closed front door.

Welcome to the neighborhood.

5

It was early morning.

My daughter was asleep. Most of the building was asleep, except for the security guard who worked the graveyard shift; he would be coming home in a few hours. Maybe I would haunt him later, kill some time until morning.

I felt restless, detached, ungrounded. Nothing new for a ghost. But tonight the feelings were especially strong, especially poignant. Something was happening, but I wasn't sure what. Being dead, after all, was still fairly new to me.

I was in a favorite part of the building—a long interior hallway that morphed into an exterior walkway. The hallway was, in effect, part interior and part exterior, and thus not subject to the regular rules and regulations that govern my haunting. Who made these rules, I didn't know, but they were there, and one such rule stated that I could not leave the confines of the building.

Anyway, I followed the interior hallway to the point where it turned into the exterior—or outer—walkway. At this juncture, I could nearly stand outside.

Nearly, but not quite.

Still, as I pretended to lean a shoulder against the hallway wall, I could almost feel the cool wind that rustled the leaves of the rustic hillside that jutted up behind the apartment complex.

As the wind picked up, a part of me wished it would take hold of me and carry me away.

And where would you go?

Good question.

The moon, hanging above the highest trees, looked cold and eternal. I felt cold and eternal. I also felt unhinged and adrift, as if the smallest breeze might blow me away.

As I continued staring up into the night sky, and as the wind continued passing straight through me, a pinprick of light appeared in the heavens above. It could have been a star, but it wasn't, and suddenly, I knew why I was feeling so unsettled.

The pinprick of light grew rapidly into something much more than a pinprick. Much, much more. And it kept growing and expanding until it had burned a hole into the sky. Golden light poured out.

It was the tunnel to heaven.

6

I had first seen the tunnel two years ago.

I had been asleep. I had been dreaming of work, my baby girl, my failed marriage, and everything in between when a half-dozen loud explosions forcibly yanked me out of my sleep and, apparently, right out of my body.

To say I was confused was an understatement.

In utter bewilderment, I found myself floating in my bedroom, floating above my body, as a man, standing in the middle of my room and holding a gun, pulled the trigger again and shot me point-blank in my chest. The explosion was loud, deafening in the confined space. But my body didn't move with the impact. I was already dead.

Hell of a bad dream.

The shooter fell to his knees and dropped his gun and buried his face in his hands. I saw that he was wearing latex gloves. His body shook as he sobbed. Eventually, he got hold of himself, picked up his gun, and stood. He looked down at my dead body. So did I. The sheet was now completely covered in blood and gleaming wetly.

He quickly left my bedroom, and a moment later, I heard my front door open and then click shut. He was gone, and I was dead.

Why he killed me, I didn't know. Why he wept, I didn't know. Who he was is still a mystery.

As I hovered above my body, I could smell my fresh blood and I could smell the gunpowder. In the distance, I could hear an ambulance coming, or perhaps the police. Someone had reported the gunshots.

I'm dreaming; this really isn't happening. I'm going to wake up any moment now.

It was then that a bright light appeared above me. I turned away from my body and looked up, and there, replacing my ceiling, was a golden tunnel. Light poured out of it and washed over me, and something close to singing reached my ears. Heartbreakingly beautiful singing. The voice of angels.

I could see people inside the tunnel. Not people, really, but spirits, souls. They were all glowing.

The light in the tunnel was inviting. I felt its pull. I *wanted* to drift up to it. I *needed* to drift up to it.

But I also felt fear. No, *terror*. If I was dead—and I was seriously suspecting that I was *not* dreaming—then God awaited beyond that golden tunnel. God and judgment and hell.

So I resisted the pull. I resisted with all my might.

And that's when I saw the beautiful dark-haired woman standing in the far corner of my bedroom.

7

She approached me slowly, smiling warmly, her hands folded together at her waist. She was wearing a white translucent gown. No, the gown wasn't translucent.

She was translucent.

Good God, I can see through her! This can't be happening.

Now she was standing before me as I hovered over my dead body. I tried standing, but I was unable to control my movements. I felt helpless and trapped.

I'm dreaming.

"No, James. You have passed on." Her voice was soothing and full of love. So much love.

"Do I know you?" I asked.

"Yes," she answered, and I saw the tears in her eyes. I *think* they were tears of joy, but I could have been wrong. I also realized that her lips weren't moving.

Yeah, this is a dream.

"I don't know what's happening to me," I said. I could hear the panic in my voice.

The woman held out her hand to me. "It's okay, James. Take my hand."

Never had I felt such love. So real and palpable. It came in wave after wave from this strange woman, washing over me, around me, *through* me.

"Take my hand, James. It's okay. Come with me. I will explain everything to you, but for now, it's time to go."

Her hand was small and elegant and seemed suffused with an inner light that appeared to reach out beyond the hand itself.

"We need to go," she calmly said again.

And with those words, the glowing tunnel above flared in intensity. But instead of taking her hand, I said, "I know you from somewhere."

She only smiled as another wave of love washed over me, engulfing me completely.

"Who are you?" I asked.

"You will remember," she said, "in time."

"You are so beautiful."

She stepped forward and held out her glowing hand. Like a Michelangelo painting, I reached down for it, and when our fingers touched, a fleeting, haunting image of the two of us flashed through my mind: she and I were in a golden field, with the sun high above. We were desperately, madly in love.

"I miss you, James," she said. "We all do. It's time for you to come home."

Something deep inside me was overjoyed by her presence, but it was buried deep beneath the confusion, the horror, and the fear.

"Don't be afraid, James," she said. "You are deeply loved."

"I've done some bad things," I said.

"I know," she said.

"I don't want to go to hell," I said.

She looked away, and now there were tears on her high cheekbones, burning like golden drops of liquid sun. She said nothing.

"Am I going to hell?" I asked. I heard the desperation in my voice.

At that moment, something started happening: she started *fading* before my eyes. "Please, James," she said, gripping me tighter. "We can be together again. Everything will be okay."

"Will it?" I asked, pulling back. "How do you know?"

"Please, James."

Frozen with fear, afraid to face what lay beyond, I didn't move. And when she disappeared altogether, the golden tunnel in the ceiling disappeared with her, and I was left alone with my own dead body.

And that's when the eternal cold set in.

* * *

The tunnel in the sky shone brightly now.

I could feel its pull, like a siren's song. Every instinct in my nonbody told me to *go to the light*. That going to the light was the natural thing to do, that it was the *right* thing to do, that it was the logical thing to do.

No, I thought. *Not yet.*

Lately, the tunnel had been appearing less frequently and its pull seemed to be diminishing. As if it were giving up on me.

Don't give up on me yet, I thought. *I need more time. Just give me a little more time.*

The light in the sky wavered. It always wavered just before it disappeared. I continued gazing up at it, continued fighting its gentle pull. Why the tunnel existed, I didn't know, but it was a part of my life now—or more accurately, a part of my *death*. Where and to whom it led, I did not know. But I suspected it led to heaven.

Or to hell.

The wind, like something curious and blind, moved over the ceramic tiles of the outdoor hallway, feeling everything, touching everything. But not me. Never me. Instead, it went *through* me. On the hillside beyond the balcony, something crashed through the trees and then scurried up the hillside. A raccoon, perhaps.

Maybe it's scared of ghosts.

When I looked up again, the tunnel was gone.

Don't give up on me, I thought. *Please.*

8

It was late afternoon, and I was standing near Pauline's sliding glass door as the setting sun angled down into her living room, splashing across the polished Pergo floors and straight through me.

I was drawing energy from the sun, which meant I was in a high-energy state. Pauline, however, wasn't in a high-energy state. She lounged languidly on her couch, and I suspected there was a strong drink in her very near future.

"You suspect right," she said, standing with considerable effort. "Hey, you're shadowing," she said as she passed by me.

Indeed, I was. I looked down, and there I was on the floor, a vague shape of a man. Gleefully, I moved my arms, and the shadow's arms moved as well.

A thrill coursed through me.

Pauline appeared a moment later with an apple martini in her hand. "I'd offer you one, love, but it's going to take more than a shadow to put it away."

"Thanks," I said. "I think."

"So why are you haunting me tonight?" she asked.

"Why? Do you have something better to do?"

"Than to hang out with a ghost? Sadly, no." She took a sip from her drink and studied me. "So tell me, honey, why are you here tonight? I sense you want to ask me something."

There were no secrets with Pauline. "I want your help to bust me out of here."

"Bust you out of where?"

"Here," I said. "The apartment building."

She set down her drink directly on her hand-painted coffee table. So much for the coaster. "And where would you like to go, Mr. Blakely?" she asked.

An image of the monastery must have been sitting heavily on my mind, because she nodded almost instantly.

"I see," she said. "So you are serious about looking into your music teacher's murder?"

"Deadly serious."

"And you think this will help save your soul?" she asked.

"It couldn't hurt," I said.

"Did it ever occur to you that it might be too late for you, James?"

"Yes."

"But you're going to go through with this anyway?"

"Yes."

She sat forward on the love seat, the springs creaking beneath her weight. She reached out and held the stem of the martini glass without actually lifting it.

"You've been dead nearly two years?" she asked.

Dates were getting fuzzy with me, but that number seemed right. "Yes," I said. "I think."

"And what, exactly, have you done during these past two years to help save your soul? And finding Mrs. Carney's lost cat doesn't count, since you were the one who spooked it in the first place."

"I found Mrs. Carney's lost cat."

"Doesn't count."

"I've been waiting for the right situation," I said.

"And you think finding your music teacher's murderer is that situation?"

I thought about that. "It feels right. I can't explain it other than that."

"It *feels* right?"

I sensed her trying to talk me out of this. I didn't want to be talked out of this. I wanted this. "I adored that woman," I said. "I want to help."

"There's one problem, James," she said. "You're earthbound to this apartment building."

"Which is why I need your help."

She sighed heavily and took a sip from her drink. "Fine. Let me ask around."

"Who will you ask?"

"I know people," she said.

"Dead people?" I asked.

"*Very* dead people."

9

A few days later, Pauline stepped through her front door and found me hovering in her kitchen. I had, admittedly, been waiting for her.

"How was your day, dear?" I asked pleasantly.

She ignored me and tossed her purse and keys on her kitchen table and headed straight for the fridge. A moment later, she emerged with a bottle of Miller Lite.

"You know," she said, "there are some people who are greeted by their mate when they first come home. Or by their kids. Or even their dogs. Me? I get a ghost."

"I could take offense at that," I said. "At least you have someone."

"I'm sorry," she said. "That was a shitty thing to say."

"I could piss on your leg, if that makes you feel any better."

"I said I'm sorry. Besides, I have good news. I might have found a way to break you out of here." She twisted off the cap to her beer and drank deeply from it. When she pulled away to breathe, she said, "I'd offer you one, but you don't have any lips."

"Very funny," I said.

"Wait till I have a few beers in me—I'll be a regular comedian."

We moved over to the couch. She curled her feet under her and looked steadily at me. "I'm going to miss you, James."

That surprised me. "That's if we can figure out a way to get me to the church. Besides, I always got the impression that I bothered you, Pauline. That since you spent the bulk of your day dealing with the dead, the last thing you wanted was to have a ghost haunting you at home."

Outside, in the parking lot below, a car alarm suddenly went off, immediately followed by the sound of running feet. Had a car alarm actually served its purpose? Pauline ignored the sound. She was silent and meditative, her thoughts closed even to me.

Finally, she said, "Yes, James, there are times when I desperately need a break from the dead, even from you. No offense."

"None taken."

"But you seem to be pretty good at discerning those times, so it's mostly not a problem."

She was staring intently at me. I wondered just how much of me she could actually see.

"I see the outline of you," she said, reading my thoughts. "I see your jawline, your cheekbones, your mouth. You have very full lips."

"*Had* very full lips," I corrected.

She ignored me. "You were a very handsome man, James. I could have loved a man like you."

"Well, I think you do a little," I said. It was meant as a joke, but my ability to joke seemed to have gone the way of my body. After all, humor was as much body language and inflection as it was content, and I didn't have much of either these days.

She studied me from over her bottle of beer, then swirled the contents, which caused frothing whitecaps to appear over the lip.

"Frothing whitecaps? You have a vivid imagination."

"It's what makes me special."

29

"Yes, you are special," she said. "And, yes, I do think I love you a little. You have proven to be a good friend and a wonderful confidant."

She stared at me some more, then drank from her beer. As she did so, I found myself trying to remember how beer tasted. *Hoppy* and *bitter* were two words that came to mind—two words that had mostly lost their meaning to me.

"Don't forget *filling, complete,* and *quenching*," said Pauline, easily following my train of thought. She finished her beer, got up from the couch, and headed over to the kitchen. She tossed the empty bottle and got herself another one. "Here, let me give you a taste."

"I don't think so," I said. I could just imagine her dumping the beer all over her kitchen floor as she tried to find my ghostly gullet.

"No," she said, "I have another idea. Come here."

I approached her nervously. What did she have in mind? I paused about halfway through the kitchen as she took a long drink from the bottle, then wet her lips slowly with her narrow tongue. She moved over to me. Or perhaps *sidled* would have been a better word. Either way, she had a fairly hungry look in her eye, one that would have caused my physical body to react a certain way, no doubt.

"Just shut up for a few seconds," she said.

"But I didn't say anything."

"Then turn off your damn brain and relax."

"I'm a ghost. How much more relaxed could I be? Besides, I don't have a brain—"

"Shh!"

Now she was standing before me. Her eyes roamed my face with interest. She reached up and touched my hair—or tried to.

"Your hair is slightly mussed," she said.

"Yeah, well, I was asleep when I died."

"I want you to do something for me," she said.

I didn't say anything. I just stood there in the kitchen, looking down at this woman I had gotten to know so well over the past two years. A woman who was my only connection to the real world.

"Shh," she hissed again. "I want you to draw energy from me. You know how to do it, and I give you my full permission. I want to see you, James. All of you."

She had never given me such permission, and rarely did I draw upon the energy of others. Not sure why I didn't; again, call it ghostly etiquette.

"Do it," she said. "And just shut up. But first..." She drank deeply from the bottle and licked her lips again. "Okay, now do it."

And so I did. I reached out and held her head in my hands. She closed her eyes and tilted her head back. Energy—her energy—crackled up my arms and through my body, spreading to all my extremities. Her eyelids fluttered wildly.

A moment later, I made a full appearance.

* * *

She opened her eyes and smiled at me—and nearly fainted. In fact, she would have fallen to the floor had I not held her up.

"Don't let go," she said.

So I continued holding her head in my milky-white hands, continued drawing energy from her.

"Kiss me," she said throatily. She opened her eyes and tried to smile—and nearly fainted again. "Do it now, you dope."

And so I did.

Holding her face in my hands, I leaned down and pressed my semisubstantial lips down onto hers. Her lips, soft and wet, were coated with a thin film of beer. As I kissed her, more energy passed from her to me. A lot more energy.

Too much.

Finally, I pulled away from her. As I did so, a thin elastic thread of ectoplasm stretched from my lips to hers and snapped off in a puff of cotton candy as I carefully lowered her to the kitchen floor.

I stepped back, and two things happened simultaneously: she slowly regained her strength, and I slowly disappeared.

But before I faded altogether, I fetched her a pillow from the couch, slipped it under her head. When she opened her eyes again, she looked up at me weakly and smiled.

"So how did the beer taste?" she asked.

I grinned down at her, licking my lips.

"Wonderful."

10

Pauline came back slowly.

Making a full appearance was rare for me. To do so, I needed the full compliance of the living. Most of the living rarely complied.

I was still reeling from the kiss. Her lips had been so soft against mine. I could still taste the alcohol on her lips. I could taste something else, too—her lipstick. And her perfume was more than just a phantasmal hint.

It was the real thing. And she had smelled so damn good.

"Thank you," she said, sitting up, blinking hard. "You were bad. I told you to kiss me, not suck the life out of me."

"My bad," I said.

She sat up on the Pergo floor and wrapped her arms around her knees. Dust bunnies, stirred up from the recent commotion, flitted across the floor like mini gray ghosts. I said nothing, although my thoughts turned to my wife, who was living two floors above us and a hallway or two down.

"You didn't cheat, silly," she said.

"Feels like cheating."

"We're just friends experimenting. Like I did back in college, only you're not a sophomore cheerleader with sexuality issues."

"Still, I should be kissing *her*," I said.

"She doesn't know you exist," said Pauline gently. "Besides, James, she remarried, remember?"

No, I hadn't remembered. These days I was forgetting more and more. Then again, perhaps that was a memory I *wanted* to forget. Good God, my wife had remarried?

I felt as if someone had sucker punched me in the gut.

Pauline stood on shaky legs. "You're going to be okay, kiddo. I promise." She headed straight to the fridge and pulled out another bottle of beer. "Now, I actually had some news to tell you."

"That is, before we got distracted," I said, and suddenly wondered why I was feeling so awful. But I couldn't remember. Something to do with my wife, I think. I shrugged off the feeling.

"That was a hell of a distraction," said Pauline.

"Did your news have something to do with me finding a way out of here?"

"Yes," she said.

"So how do we do it?" I asked.

She grinned at me. "I'm going to need a pair of your socks."

11

It was past midnight, and my daughter was sleeping soundly.

I stepped into her bedroom through her closet door, noting that she appeared to have a new winter coat inside the closet, although I couldn't quite remember if it was new or not. At any rate, it certainly seemed new.

Damned memory.

She was sleeping on her back, with her head turned slightly toward me. Thanks to a nearly full moon, the light inside her room was especially bright.

I noted that she had recently added a life-size poster of Kobe Bryant slam-dunking a basketball, feet hovering unnaturally above the court, tongue sticking out, face contorted in the sweaty throes of competition. I was uncomfortable with my nine-year-old daughter having a poster of anyone in the sweaty throes of *anything.*

She was growing up.

I hated that.

And she was doing so with a new daddy now. The man himself was kind enough, yes, although he really didn't give her enough time or attention. She was always an afterthought, always an obligation, and she deserved much better. So much better.

She deserved *me.*

"I'm doing my best, baby doll," I said to her sleeping figure.

As I spoke, her aura shifted toward me, as it always did. It had been undulating softly in sleep, and now suddenly crackled with energy. The red lapping flames flared up toward me before dissipating into puffs of fuchsia-tinted smoke.

I sat next to her. "Hi, baby," I said. "You know I'm here, don't you?"

Her aura shifted colors. The red was now interlaced with wisps of blue steel.

"What are you dreaming about?" I asked softly.

More blue wisps penetrated the red. She was awakening. The colors together were beautiful. A phantasmagoric rainbow, perhaps made more beautiful because they were emitting from my daughter. Either way, I could watch them all night, and sometimes I did.

"I don't remember what I was dreaming about, Daddy," she said sleepily.

The blue bands continued to weave through the red, and now there seemed to be some orange and yellow in there, too. The colors of her mood. She was excited. Her aura also retracted a little, quieting down, much the same way as an excited puppy will eventually calm down. As she lay there on her side, eyes closed, she appeared to be asleep, but the blue in her aura gave her away. The blue meant she was semiconscious. Or rather, a *part* of her was semiconscious and very much aware of me.

"You like Kobe, eh?" I said.

She giggled. "Yes! Everyone does!"

"Because he's such a great basketball player?"

"No!" she said, laughing. "Because he's so cute!"

"Oh, brother," I said.

She giggled some more.

I said, "You're too young to think boys are cute."

"He's not a boy. He's a man."

"Okay, you are *definitely* too young to think men are cute."

"Oh, *Dad*. I know!"

We were quiet some more. The silver moonlight and reddish alarm clock light fused together to give her face a sort of pinkish glow, a face that was indeed losing some of its chubbiness. Her cheekbones were making an appearance. And thanks to her mother, she was going to be beautiful.

"Daddy needs your help," I said.

Her aura flared immediately, snapping and crackling like a fire-breathing dragon. She shifted in her sleep, and her eyelids fluttered briefly, as if she might fully awaken. She spoke excitedly. "Anything for you, Daddy! What do you need?"

I paused. This was going to be hard. "Daddy needs his scarf back."

"Your scarf?" she asked, confused.

"Yes."

Her aura receded like a blue-and-red tide. Some of the crimson in it flared to green, and I knew this was the color of her sadness. She loved that scarf and wore it all the time, even when the weather didn't permit.

"Of course, Daddy," she said. "I would give you anything. Are you cold?"

Daddy is always cold, I wanted to say. Instead, I said, "Yes, baby, a little."

"You can have it, Daddy."

"Thank you, angel."

We were silent some more, and the dull green in her aura flashed brilliantly emerald and then was gone, replaced with something brown. I knew this to be the color of her resolve. Her strength.

"I don't want you to be cold, Daddy."

"You are a good girl."

I told her exactly what I needed for her to do next, and she did what I asked, operating in a semihypnotic state. She pushed aside her covers, got up from the bed, and went over to her dresser. She pulled open the top drawer, rummaged through it briefly, and pulled out the red scarf, now well worn. It wasn't socks, as Pauline had requested, but it would do. Next, she walked to her bedroom door, opened it, and stepped out into the hallway. I drifted through her room and followed her. She moved surprisingly fast for someone walking with her eyes shut. Then again, the muscle memory was there, and her aura reached out before her, guiding the way.

The spirit always knows the way.

She opened the front door to the apartment and wrapped the scarf around the doorknob, where Pauline would collect it early the next morning.

She shut the door again, locked it, and headed back to her bedroom, deftly avoiding the corner of the kitchen table. She shut the bedroom door and crawled back into bed. I could see the tears on her cheeks. She loved that scarf.

"You are a good girl," I said.

"I don't want you to be cold, Daddy."

"I love you, baby. Now, get some sleep."

12

I had good days in death, and I had bad days in death.

This was a bad day.

"Excuse me, sir," I said. "Can you help me? I think I'm lost."

But the man wearing the shabby seersucker coat ignored me. His head and shoulders were wet, and the umbrella he was carrying was dripping rainwater all over the polished marble floor. He was leaving a slippery—and dangerous—trail down the center of the hallway. Not only did he care little for others' welfare, the bastard was also ignoring me.

I picked up my pace and tapped him on the shoulder. At least, I *think* I tapped him on the shoulder.

Sweet Jesus, did my finger just pass through his shoulder? Of course not. I'm seeing things.

"Excuse me, sir?" I said again.

But he kept moving briskly through the hallway. I moved briskly, too, directly behind him. His leather hiking boots squeaked along the floor. I didn't squeak at all.

"Hey," I said, "why won't you—"

And then he stopped suddenly and I nearly ran into him. Actually, I *did* run into him. Or, rather, I *should have* run into him. Instead, I went *through* him.

Stunned, I stepped back. The man was shivering now, nearly uncontrollably. The hair on the back of his neck was standing on end.

"Excuse me," I said again, completely shaken. "I think I'm lost."

His back was still to me. He cocked his head to one side and appeared to be listening. Then slowly—very slowly—he turned around and looked straight at me.

Well, sort of.

Actually, his eyes had that sort of glazed, unfocused look that people get when they're staring off into space.

Or looking through you.

"Sir?" I said again.

He continued staring through me for another beat or two, then frowned and turned and started squeaking down the hallway again.

I watched him go. He paused outside a door, fished for a bundle of keys in his pocket, sought one out, and inserted it into the lock. He opened the door and was gone in an instant, and I was left standing in the hallway alone.

What the hell?

I turned slowly. I realized, with some alarm, that nothing looked familiar. The hallway was covered in mirrors. I stopped turning and faced one such mirror.

There was nothing *in* the mirror.

I wasn't in the mirror!

Maybe they weren't mirrors. I walked over to it, reached out a finger to touch it, and…My finger passed straight through the mirror as if it weren't there.

No, a voice in my head said. *It's you who isn't here.*

I next looked at my hand. It was there, true, but I could actually see through it. *Through my own hand.*

Jesus!

I turned in circles, panicking. Where was I? The mirrored hallway...the smooth granite floor...the polished wooden ceiling fans...

I knew this place. I had been here before.

Think!

I tried to think, but there was no memory at all of who I was or why I was here. Fear gripped me. Pure, unadulterated fear. And now I found myself backing away—and into the mirrored wall behind me.

And backing *through* it.

In a blind panic, I found myself running down the hallway of mirrors. I turned wildly around a corner and was about to head outside along what appeared to be a connecting outdoor walkway—and slammed headlong into something invisible, and hard.

I stumbled backward, disoriented, thoroughly confused. I reached for a stucco column to support myself, but my hand passed straight through it, too.

Please, God, let this be a bad dream.

I staggered, found my balance. What the hell had I hit? I didn't know, but now I inched forward slowly, reaching out my hand cautiously before me. Beyond the railing of the hallway was a steep hill covered in dense shrubs. A small wind touched me—and then promptly passed straight through me.

I'm dreaming, I thought. *I have to be dreaming.*

I took another step, then another, and my outstretched hand touched *something*. Something hot and electrified. I recoiled instantly.

Jesus, what the hell was that?

Suddenly, an image flashed in my thoughts, of a man being shot to death in his sleep. The man looked familiar. Very familiar. I was suddenly certain I knew who this man was.

But my brain wasn't working, refused to click into gear, refused to draw up any memories at all.

Another flashing image. A very cute little girl. My heart instantly warmed. *My* girl. Yes, that was *my* girl.

But I couldn't remember her name or even if she was a little girl anymore. More images. A woman I knew. An apartment I knew. Gunshots. Flashes of light. Images of a golden tunnel in the sky.

I continued backing away from the outside walkway, continued backing away from the invisible barrier that impeded me. And I backed straight through a stucco wall, to find myself surrounded by mops and brooms and buckets and cleaning agents. A janitor's closet.

Disoriented and confused, I found myself falling. Straight through the floor.

Down, down.

Screaming.

13

I dropped into an apartment.

Inside, flashing by me in a blur, were a woman and a toddler playing near the TV. The toddler turned its little head, saw me, and pointed excitedly with a chubby finger...

But I was already falling down through the hardwood floor. I instinctively covered my face and screamed—and passed straight through into another room.

This one was dark and vacant. I braced myself for the coming floor, expecting to pass right through it, as I had done the others...

But this time I hit the floor hard and something close to pain coursed through me. Or was it the memory of pain? I lay there for a moment, scared and completely bewildered, and realized I wasn't in pain at all.

"They're all memories," said a voice behind me. "You cannot feel pain, James. Not really, not the way you used to. But you *remember* how it felt, and sometimes that's good enough."

I looked up from the ground where I lay, and there stood an angel across the dark room, glowing softly. I slowly found my feet.

"I'm not an angel," she said, blushing slightly, the color red rippling through her silvery, ethereal glow. "But I'm honored you think so."

"You just read my thoughts," I said, backing away.

"Yes, and you're reading mine, James."

Indeed, her mouth never moved, yet I heard her words perfectly clearly.

"Who are you?" I asked.

"Just a friend," she said, although she sounded mildly hurt. Her incandescent glow now rippled with green.

I was in what appeared to be a storeroom, filled with dismantled sinks, dented trash cans, toilets, and rows and rows of unused lumber.

"Why did I stop falling in here?"

"Because you are earthbound to this building, James, and as long as this building stands, you will never leave it. And should this building ever be destroyed, you are bound to the empty lot. For all eternity."

"I don't understand," I said, and felt the rush of fear all over again.

"Yes, you do, James. Make yourself understand—it's important that you do."

"Why do you keep calling me James?"

"Because that's your name."

I suddenly wanted to run. I wanted to be anywhere but here in this creepy room.

"Anywhere but here?" she said, reading my thoughts. "I could take offense at that, James."

"No offense, it's just that—"

"You're scared."

"Yes."

She continued hovering before me and glowing serenely. She was the most beautiful woman I had ever seen. And at that thought, she smiled warmly at me, and in her smile, there was so much love that I nearly broke down in tears.

"Why do you look at me like that?" I asked.

She did not answer me; instead, she continued smiling, continued sending me wave after wave of love.

"Why do you love me so much?" I asked. "I don't know you."

But her smile never wavered. I thought of the dead man I had seen in the vision, the man who had been shot to death. I looked down at my body now, at my chest and stomach. Both were dotted with bullet wounds. "I'm the dead man in the vision," I said.

She continued saying nothing, but something horrible started happening. She started fading.

"And the girl in my vision is my daughter," I cried out to her.

She smiled and faded and said nothing.

"And I'm dead," I said.

But she was already gone.

And in the empty silence and darkness of the storage room, I found myself looking at my own glowing hands. Hands that I could actually see through. "And my name is James," I said to the emptiness.

And with horrific clarity, I remembered everything in a rush of ghastly memories, and I found myself on my knees, weeping molten tears that fell from my cheeks and shriveled and dissipated before they hit the cold concrete floor.

14

Pauline was sitting on her couch with her legs stretched out before her. She was drinking a cosmopolitan and seemed to be enjoying it.

"It's heavenly," she said. "By the way, I hid the scarf in the church today."

"Thank you, Pauline."

"Thank your daughter, too. She gave up her scarf for you."

"I love her more than you know."

"Oh, I know," she said.

"Yeah, I suppose you would know."

In death, I had known only the apartment, known only its mirrored hallways, its many residents, its empty storerooms, and the forgotten nooks and crannies that most residents didn't know—or cared to know—existed.

This was my home. This was my haunt in more ways than one. It was all I'd known in death. And sometimes, this was all I remembered, too.

Pauline was polite enough to let me work through my anxiety without comment. I sat on the coffee table across from her. The sitting, of course, was just an illusion. I simply made the motion of sitting. I am, after all, nothing but energy.

"You are more than energy," she said.

"How much of me can you really see?" I asked.

"I can see enough of you. The rest I fill in with my imagination."

She then got up from the couch and sat next to me on the coffee table. I could sense the heat coming off her body but not really feel it. She opened her hand and held it out to me.

"Take it," she said.

I did my best to hold on to hers, and we sat there like that in silence, holding hands. Outside, a dog barked. Inside, a medium and a ghost were holding hands. She turned her face and I saw that there were tears on her cheeks. I put my arm around her and she unconsciously shivered. The dog continued barking and we continued hugging and holding hands.

15

It was late and she was asleep.

Her aura had shifted toward me, but this time, I kept my distance.

Let her sleep, I thought. *Leave her be.*

A very small part of me realized that I had been selfish by coming in here and disturbing her sleep, causing her unknown psychosomatic problems in her waking life.

She rolled over now, and her angelic face angled toward me. Her eyelids fluttered. Her aura, now a soft pink with occasional flashes of red, snapped at me like tiny, fiery bullwhips.

Do it now. Before she wakes.

As Pauline had instructed, I closed my eyes, which, somehow, I could still do. I held the image of the red scarf in my thoughts. I visualized it as clearly as I could. I saw myself touching it, holding it. I visualized it as I used to wear it: around my neck, flapping in the wind behind me as if I were a WWI fighter pilot.

Focus.

Focus on the scarf.

And so I did. I saw it around my neck, could feel it in my hands, remembered the cozy warmth it had provided me in days past, days I could no longer remember.

Focus.

In my mind's eye, the scarf seemed to solidify, seemed to coalesce into something real, something more than thought, something more than memory.

When I opened my eyes again, there it was.

In my hands.

The red scarf.

In shock, I looked up and immediately felt a wave of dizziness. I was not expecting to see what I saw before me. I had been expecting to see my daughter's room.

Instead, I found myself standing in a cavernous church cathedral.

16

I released my hold on the scarf, which had been tucked deep into the cushions of a church pew.

I took in my surroundings. I was in a church nave. And not just any nave. It was the church of my youth, where I had gone to school for so many years of my life, where, among other things, my fear of God had been born.

A hell of a fear.

It was the middle of the night, and the church was empty—and creepy. Even for a ghost. I drifted out to the center aisle and stopped there. The ceiling was high and arched and vast. Massive stained-glass windows circled the cavernous room, each depicting popular scenes from the Bible: David leading his flock, Jesus breaking bread, Moses and his commandments, Enoch riding a fiery dervish into the heavens.

At the back of the church, hanging high above the sanctuary, was a bloody, lifelike statue of Jesus Christ suspended from the cross. Too lifelike. The sculptor had gone a little crazy with the blood, which poured from many open wounds. Anyone looking up at the statue couldn't help but be powerfully struck by Christ's ultimate sacrifice for our sins.

I remembered the statue. It had given me nightmares when I was a child. I looked away from it now.

I knew the building had once been an old monastery, and I knew the monastery had a rich cultural history—and a bloody one, too. There had, in fact, been many tragedies. None of which I could remember now—that is, except this latest one.

The murder of my music teacher.

Who would kill her? And why kill her here, at school, within this very cathedral? According to the newspaper article—which Pauline had located and recently read to me *twice*—the police had found no motive and very few clues.

I spied the piano from across the vast cathedral, gleaming dully, sitting high on the raised dais.

The very piano she had been strangled on.

I drifted toward it, down the center aisle. I recalled that the church was popular for weddings. Down this very aisle many brides had walked arm in arm with their fathers before being given away. I would never give my daughter away. Ever.

As a crushing sadness threatened to overcome me, I continued down the center aisle toward the raised stage. And as I did so, I realized I wasn't alone.

Here be ghosts.

17

I was about halfway down the aisle, approaching the raised sanctuary, with its altar and lectern and pulpit, when a figure stepped out from behind a velvet curtain to my right.

Or, rather, stepped *through* the curtain.

It was a child, and he stood there watching me, one finger raised to his lip. He was glowing softly. If not for the fact that I could see through him or that he was pulsating with his own inner luminosity, he would have looked like any other precocious child.

Granted, one had to ignore the mortal wound in his head and the transparent blood that stained his freshly ironed dress shirt. Except, I couldn't ignore it.

Sweet Jesus.

Ghosts and color don't exactly mix, and so the bloodstain on his shirt was really just a splash of silver, which spread all the way down to his navel. Sweet Jesus…What had happened to him? I knew my own ethereal body was covered in similar splotches—thirteen gunshot wounds, to be exact.

The child watched me some more, rising and falling gently as if adrift on some unseen, unfelt current.

I moved closer to him.

"What's your name?" I asked from a few pews away, keeping my distance.

He didn't answer, just continued to bob gently on the noncurrents of nonspace. I drifted closer still.

I said, "My name is..." but I suddenly had to stop and think. Panic surged through me. What the hell was my name? Jim? Jack? No, not quite. James? *Yes, James!*

"My name is James," I said.

I think.

He watched me some more, then finally spoke, his voice small and hesitant, barely reaching my ears. "I don't remember my name, mister."

I nodded. "That's okay. Sometimes I don't remember mine, either."

He next surprised me by confidently and boldly moving toward me, drifting straight through the pews. Perhaps he sensed a friend. As he came toward me, his slightly mussed hair never moved—and would never move again. And neither would mine, no matter how hard the wind might blow.

His cheeks were still chubby, and I saw the ghostly hint of freckles. His eyes were bright. The brutal damage to his head made me want to look away, but I forced myself not to. Now, of course, he did not feel the pain, just as I did not feel the bloody wounds that dotted me from head to toe.

And, perhaps most amazingly, he looked familiar.

I think.

"You got all shot up," said the boy.

"Yes," I said.

"Were you bad, too?"

"Maybe," I said. "I don't remember."

"I was bad and I had to die."

Sweet, sweet Jesus.

"Why didn't you go to heaven?" I asked.

"Daddy says there is no heaven," he answered.

"And you believe your daddy?" I asked, surprised, since I had found the boy in a church, after all.

"Oh, yes!"

"Do you have any brothers or sisters?"

He paused long and hard. "I think so, yes. A brother."

"Do you have a mommy?" I asked.

"Yes."

And then he did something I was completely unprepared for. He burst into tears and threw his little arms around my waist and hugged me hard, burying his nose in my hip. His deep shudders rippled through me as he cried long and hard.

I put my arm hesitantly around him. "You miss your mommy, don't you?"

"I want to go home," he said, his voice muffled. "Please help me go home, mister."

18

We sat together in the front pew.

The image of Jesus Christ hovered above us in all its contorted, bloody glory. The boy rested his wounded head on my shoulder. From this angle, I could look down into his broken skull. I averted my eyes.

I wasn't sure what to say to him or how to console him. I was certain that his lack of belief in the afterlife was keeping him grounded to the church, the place of his death.

So I asked the obvious question: "If you don't believe in heaven, then why did you go to church?"

He wiped his nose, although there was nothing running from it. Strictly a human habit. "Mommy made us go."

"Us?"

"Yes, me and my brother."

"I see. But your dad didn't believe."

He screwed up his little face. "I can't really remember anymore, mister. But that sounds about right."

"So your teachers taught you one thing, and when you came home, your dad taught you another. And you believed your dad, because he's your dad."

The boy nodded eagerly, but I was certain I had lost him, and I was also certain that he had lost the specifics of his own life, just as I was losing the specifics of mine. Luckily, talking often to Pauline—about my life, about my past—helped me remember who I was. I suspected the boy didn't have the benefit of a powerful medium. The boy, for all intents and purposes, had been completely forgotten.

"Who killed you?" I asked.

"Some boys. Older boys. Big boys."

"Why did they kill you?" I asked.

The little boy shrugged. "I don't remember. But I did something bad. They kept telling me I was a bad boy and that I deserved to fall."

To fall?

Suddenly, a series of violent, flashing images—all coming from the boy's own memory—came to me. As they did so, the boy began rocking back and forth on the pew.

Two older boys, both dressed in traditional Catholic uniforms— black slacks, white button-up short-sleeve shirts—were laughing at him. The images were distorted. They appeared in the boy's thoughts rapidly and probably out of order, as if a film editor had gotten a movie's sequence all mixed up:

An image of the older boys laughing at him...

Being dragged up a dark flight of steep stairs...

Boys and girls playing on the playground...

Two boys waving him over to a drinking fountain...

Being hauled through a dark doorway...

Hanging over a wooden beam—a rafter...

Looking down to the sanctuary far below...

Children skipping rope outside...

Kicking and screaming, begging for forgiveness...

One of the older boys screaming that something had been stolen. Blaming the little boy...

Children running to a drinking fountain, jostling to be first in line...
The older boys reaching down for the falling boy, horror on their faces...
The altar rapidly approaching below...
Rapidly...
Blackness.
And then the boy, confused and terrified, hovering over his own broken, dead body, blood everywhere...
The older boys appearing now at ground level, out of breath, their faces pale with shock and horror...
And then they are running, dashing through the church...

* * *

The boy stopped rocking next to me. I looked at him and found him absently probing his crushed skull, slipping his fingers inside the deep gash.

Sweet Jesus.

"Jesus was just a man," said the boy, picking up on my thoughts. "He wasn't really God. That's what my daddy says."

I nodded, and we were quiet some more. The boy's thoughts were mostly quiet, although occasionally a very old woman would appear in them. I sensed love radiating from her, and so did the boy, but he was confused and did not remember her.

"I'm sorry you died," I said.

"It's okay. I mostly don't remember it. Just when I'm reminded of it."

"I'm sorry that I reminded you."

"It's okay," he said again. "Sometimes it feels like it happened to someone else, you know? Like I'm remembering a movie or someone else's memories. Does that ever happen to you?"

I nodded. I knew what he was talking about. Probably what Alzheimer's patients dealt with. A detachment from one's own memories. Distrust of one's own memories.

A horrible, horrible feeling.

And since we were already in a gloomy state, I decided to go ahead and get this over with, and pushed forward. "There was a teacher killed in this room," I said. "I think this happened a few weeks ago, but I'm not sure. Maybe shorter, maybe longer."

"Yes," said the boy eagerly. "She was my music teacher."

"Mine, too," I said.

"A man killed her," he said, nodding.

"A man?"

"Yes."

"Did you..." I paused. "Did you watch the man kill her?"

He nodded again. "Yes. I saw everything."

Now images of her murder came flashing into his mind. And because her murder was recent, the images were more concrete and vivid, and the sequence seemed to be relatively in order.

And through the boy's memory, I saw it all unfold...

19

My ex-music teacher—and neither of us can remember her name—is sitting at the piano in what appears to be late-morning light, judging by the explosion of color that angles down through the stained-glass windows above. The cavernous chapel is empty; her music fills the entire room.

I sense the boy's love for music. Or, rather, her music. I also sense that he listens to her each and every morning.

This morning is no different. He watches her from the front pew, but she is oblivious to his presence.

A sudden, rapid shift in perspective...

Now he's sitting next to her on the bench, pretending to play alongside her. She hums softly to herself, her long fingers flying nimbly over the keys, sitting straight as a board, as she always taught me to do. I could almost—almost—smell her strong perfume. Always too strong and always a bit overwhelming.

As she plays, she cocks her head to one side, as if listening for something, and then smiles to herself. Her lips move, and she forms a single word. A name, in fact.

"Jacob," she says quietly.

And now she's referring to the little boy sitting next to her. She senses him, feels him. She smiles again.

The boy's name is Jacob.

* * *

The boy picked up on my thoughts and turned to me excitedly. "My name is Jacob?"

"I think it might be," I said. "But I could be wrong. Does it sound right to you?"

He screwed up his little face, then started nodding. "Yeah, my name is Jacob. I'm sure of it." He sat back, pleased, then snapped his head around and looked at me. "Hey, mister, what's my name again?"

"Jacob," I said.

"Jacob," he said again. "Will you help me remember my name?"

"Yes," I said. "As best I can."

He smiled and clapped his hands and said his name over and over again.

"Jacob," I said gently, "can we continue with the story?"

I didn't want to make the boy relive such a horrible memory, especially since I knew something bad was about to happen to our music teacher.

"Yes," said Jacob, reading my thoughts. "Very, very bad."

But I was here for a reason. What that reason was remained to be seen. I had to know.

"Are you okay remembering all this bad stuff?" I asked him.

He nodded, and as he did so, I heard him whispering his name over and over. I slipped back into his memory, and the story continued...

20

From behind the music teacher comes a noise, a cough, someone clearing his throat.

Startled, she turns. So does Jacob. And since I'm seeing all this through the boy's eyes, so do I. A man is standing there in the center aisle, holding a gun loosely at his side, head cocked, staring oddly at the music teacher. He sports thick eyebrows, curly black hair, and impossibly bloodshot eyes.

It takes me only a second or two to dredge up the memory of my own murder—in particular, the memory of my killer looking oddly at me from the doorway, head cocked, holding his pistol loosely at his side.

Perhaps even the same pistol.

The man is also my killer.

* * *

He is speaking to the music teacher, but the boy misses most of the exchange, although I do make out "Keep quiet" and "No one gets hurt" and "Give me the…"

But Jacob misses the last word. He also misses nearly everything the music teacher says in response. The man, apparently not liking her response, suddenly points the gun at her.

And that's when she screams.

The man pounces, hurling himself up the stage. Jacob screams, too. Images flash and blur, like a camera rolling down a flight of stairs. I have no clue what's happening next, but I hear grunts and cries and banging.

When things stabilize, when the dust settles, so to speak, I see the man is now sitting on top of the music teacher as she thrashes wildly beneath, fighting and clawing.

Jacob fights, too, pounding the man furiously with tiny fists that pass harmlessly through his back. Apparently, a ghost boy and an old lady are no match for the man, as he hunches his shoulders and puts more weight into whatever it is he's doing to her.

The motherfucker is choking the life out of her. That's what he's doing.

This goes on for perhaps another minute: the boy pounding, the man hunched, me watching in helpless frustration. What happens next is surprising, but not unexpected.

While the teacher's physical body still fights her attacker, her spirit, an exact replica of the teacher herself, rises from the floor and floats a few feet above the scene. Her beautifully glowing spirit looks, to say the least, completely bewildered. I know the feeling. Below, her physical self is finally succumbing to her killer. Interestingly, her spirit was released prior to physical death.

Her spirit then looks straight ahead—and straight into Jacob's eyes. Both recoil. Her mouth opens, and various shades of gold ripple through her ethereal body. Jacob backs away as a bright light appears in the ceiling above. He looks up.

It's the tunnel.

Unaware of the events unfolding around him, the killer sits back and sucks wind. Apparently, it's hard work strangling the life out of someone.

Appearing from the stage to Jacob's left, like a troupe of heavenly actors, are a dozen or so beautifully serene and loving spirits. From them, a kindly old woman steps forward across the carpeted dais. The recognition in our teacher's eyes is instant, and immediately, her fear and confusion abate. The older woman, I can see, looks similar to our piano teacher, but younger. A sister, perhaps? I don't know, but after hugging deeply and chatting briefly, they rise together to the tunnel above.

Jacob scurries behind the altar and shuts his eyes. After an unknown amount of time, he opens his eyes and peers around the altar, but the spirits are all gone, including that of his music teacher.

Jacob is now alone with the killer.

21

The killer moves quickly.

He repositions the piano bench, which has toppled over in the melee, then moves over to the body. He struggles mightily as he lifts her, but he's a determined killer, and soon he has her back in a sitting position on the bench. He gently lays her face down on the ivory keys, closes her eyes, and folds her hands in her lap. I see that there is fresh blood beneath her nails. The killer's DNA. Something for the police to chew on. Good.

Now he reaches around her neck—the same neck he has just choked the life out of—and unclasps something. A necklace? Good God, is he just a common thief?

Not quite. The necklace has something dangling from it.

A key.

And like a cannon shot, Jacob suddenly bursts from behind the altar and launches himself onto the killer's back, kicking and screaming and punching. Although he never materializes—and I sense the boy doesn't quite know how to materialize—Jacob somehow manages to make his presence known. The killer, who was about to turn around, suddenly pauses and shivers and looks warily over his shoulder.

What happens next, admittedly, shocks even me.

The killer whispers a name—a name framed as a question: "Jacob?"

The boy, angry and spitting mad, doesn't catch his own name being whispered. But I do.

The killer pauses a moment longer, listening, waiting, then shakes his head, and now he's moving again, quickly. Jacob, still screaming, moves with him, following him around the piano and over to a side door near the raised stage. The killer uses his freshly stolen key, inserts it into the doorknob, and turns. The door opens. He steps inside, and Jacob follows right behind.

A single overhead lightbulb illuminates a small storage room packed to overflowing with all sorts of church and musical supplies: choir gowns, hymnbooks, a stack of tambourines, and what appears to be a very old drum set. The killer heads straight for the far corner of the room. There, he moves aside a vacuum cleaner and drops to his knees and fishes around inside his jacket pocket until he comes up with a screwdriver. There's a rusted air vent located at the bottom of the wall directly in front of him, and he sets to work unscrewing it, his rapid breathing filling the small room, echoing. Sweat drips from the tip of his nose. Once he gets the screws out, he moves aside the vent and reaches deep inside the dark hole in the wall.

Panic flashes across his face.

And then he smiles. He pulls something out. Something small and dark and square and covered in dust. He quickly screws the vent back into place, returns the vacuum, steps over to the room's single lightbulb. There, he examines the square object under the dim light—luckily, so does Jacob.

It's a very old leather wallet.

The killer opens it—and smiles again. Inside are many green bills. He removes them, shoves them in his front jeans pocket. Next, *he moves quickly to the rear of the storage room and finds a suitably forgotten cardboard box stuffed with black cables and shoves the wallet deep within.*

He turns, steps straight through Jacob, and shivering, exits the room.

22

Back in the sanctuary, the killer stops behind the dead woman. For the briefest of moments, I see remorse cross his bloodshot eyes, and as the man stands there staring down at her—and taking a phenomenal risk at being caught, I feel—little Jacob does something unexpected.

The boy moves around him and faces him, then reaches up and gently touches the deep wounds on the man's face—fresh wounds from our piano teacher's nails.

The moment Jacob touches him, the killer shivers, and the hairs on his forearms stand on end.

"Eli?" Jacob whispers, so low that no mortal could have possibly heard it, and yet the killer reacts instantly. He snaps his head up and looks directly into Jacob's eyes.

The two stare at each other. And because I'm reliving all of this through Jacob's memory—and thus seeing what he's seeing—I feel as if the killer is looking directly at me, too.

The name Eli strikes a chord in me, too; it pulls at a distant, forgotten memory.

Jesus, what's going on here?

But I don't have time to contemplate it, as the killer next shakes his head and yanks himself out of whatever drug-induced reverie he thinks he's in.

He heads straight to the altar.

Once there, he uses the same key to open a back panel. I know immediately what he's after: the church's treasured sacraments. Jacob watches quietly as the man removes a large plastic trash bag from inside his jacket and begins shoveling in the ornate crosses, jewel-encrusted goblets, and golden communion plates. All would fetch a pretty penny on the black market—and all should keep him high for months.

When finished, he ties off the bag and heads back behind the pulpit. And looks up. Directly above him is the massive statue of Jesus Christ hanging grotesquely from the cross.

Is the killer asking for forgiveness? Is he praying? Is he perhaps mocking the Lord?

None of the above.

Indeed, he appears to be looking at what is hanging just beneath the crucifix. It's a massive oil painting depicting Christ's arrest on the Mount of Olives. Massive and old. And probably worth a fortune.

Since when do junkies have a taste for art? Perhaps junkies looking for something—anything—to pay for their next fix.

And I thought I was going to hell.

It's a big painting and would take a lot of work for him to remove it, but the killer seems undaunted. He reaches up for it, and just as he does, something moves quickly to his left. Something dark and swift. A moving shadow, in fact. But Jacob doesn't see it, or perhaps chooses to ignore it, and so I lose my chance to see what, if anything, it is.

But something seems to be out there, moving.

The killer doesn't see it and continues reaching up, and just as his fingertips touch the ornate frame, something happens.

Unfortunately, the next few images are a blur.

In one of them, I see a very menacing red-eyed shadow rise up from the painting itself. In the next, the killer is beating a hasty retreat out of the church, his sack of stolen loot swung over his shoulder like that of a murderous Santa Claus. The anti-Santa. He looks back once, terror on his face, then quickly disappears through a side door and out into what appears to be a courtyard, complete with a gurgling fountain.

Jacob watches him go. Whatever spooked the killer doesn't seem to affect the boy, who simply turns and looks back at his dead music teacher, who's still propped up on the piano bench.

The boy floats over and lays his head on her unmoving shoulder.

* * *

Jacob and I sat together in silence.

The church itself was completely devoid of noise. Not even a creak. The structure had long ago settled into place.

After a while, I said, "You miss your music teacher, don't you?"

"She played for me every day," he said. "She would say my name and play me songs, and sometimes she would sing for me, too. She knew I was here."

We continued sitting together in the pew. The nave was empty and quiet and eternal. The boy inhaled, taking a pseudobreath, and rested his wounded head against my own bloodied shoulder, much as he had done with his piano teacher.

I put my arm around him, and we sat like that until dawn.

23

It was early morning.

I was alone in one of the church's administrative offices, gazing out a partially open window. It was one of those windows that had to be cranked open. I didn't do the cranking. Such cranking was probably beyond anything I could do in this form, anyway. Now, through the gap in the frosted-glass window, I could see the branches of an oak tree swaying in the early-morning wind. A bird or two flitted by.

A maintenance worker had come by earlier. He'd looked spooked as hell. He *should* be spooked. Here be ghosts.

Speaking of ghosts, Jacob was off roaming the nave alone. Or, as some would call it, haunting it. I had slipped away to explore my new home, although much of it was already familiar to me. Call it more of a reacquaintance.

The parking lot beyond the window was mostly empty, but it was still early. Only the maintenance man was out and about; of course, I was out and about, too, but then again, I never slept, either.

It's hard to sleep when you're living a nightmare.

Now, as I gazed out the window, I tried to recall what it was like to sleep. I knew I had enjoyed it. In fact, I remembered that sleeping in had been a rare luxury, one that I had indulged in whenever I could. Now, eternally awake, I wondered *why* I had enjoyed it so much. What had been the appeal?

I couldn't remember.

I shut my eyes, trying to remember what sleep had been like, and behind my closed lids was a churning sea of eternal blackness streaked with scattered memories and flashes of light and a horrific sense of continuously falling. I snapped my eyes open.

There was no rest for me.

Let's think about something else.

I knew who the piano teacher's killer was. Jacob had called him Eli. (And I made myself constantly repeat the name, as I did not want to forget it.) Later, when I had questioned Jacob about the name, he could not recall saying it and was adamant that he did not know who the killer was.

I still doubted that this Eli had meant to kill our piano teacher, probably assumed she would see the gun and simply give up the key.

Instead, she screamed bloody murder.

And his reaction was to quiet her. And quiet her he did, strangling the life out of her.

Then again, maybe I was wrong. Maybe his intent was to kill her all along. Maybe. But I doubted it. He had also been high on something, which accounted for his bloodshot eyes, and that something would have clouded his judgment.

Just a crackhead in need of his next fix—and in need of some extra money.

Which made me wonder, had Eli been high on something when he killed *me*? I thought back to my own death, to the look on Eli's face as he stood over my dead body. Yeah, he was definitely high on something, or drunk. Perhaps both.

The morning sun was making its appearance. Pigeons flashed across the window and into the brightening sky. I heard cars moving down a distant street, and one or two of them pulled into the church parking lot.

One thing was certain: Eli was affiliated with the church somehow, either as a worker or as a parishioner. *Something.* He'd known about the key and the wallet and when to strike—in particular, when the piano teacher would be alone in the chapel.

Perhaps he had once been a student here, too, like Jacob and me.

I thought of the two names: Eli and Jacob. Both names were biblical, and both were from the Old Testament. More importantly, both rang a tantalizing bell within me.

So what was my next step?

Easy. Find out who the hell Eli is.

24

As the early morning turned into midmorning, I searched the church and its connecting school for any signs of the killer.

I suspected Eli probably wasn't a teacher here—especially with all signs pointing to a serious drug problem—but he could have worked in other areas of the school: security, maintenance, administration.

I drifted in and out of classrooms and offices and hallways. I came across many people, of course, but none of them was Eli, which didn't surprise me. Any principal worth his or her salt wouldn't let an obvious addict around the kids. Unless said obvious addict was an old pro at hiding signs of his addiction.

Except, Eli *wasn't* an old pro. He was just a scumbag user with a disgusting habit, a user who was willing to kill an innocent woman to get his hands on a few bucks.

And he was willing to kill me, too.

So how had Eli known about the wallet? I didn't know. At least not yet.

Although I missed my daughter, I was admittedly glad to get out of my apartment complex and see some new sights, new people—

I suddenly stopped in mid-drift.

Jesus, what's her name?

73

Panic washed over me. Literally. I could see my own ethereal body ripple with the effect.

Her name, dammit! What is her name? Maddie? Mandy! It's Mandy!

Relieved, I continued down the hallway, repeating her name over and over...

And over.

*   *   *

The school was adjacent to the cathedral and thus, being part of the same building, permitted me ghostly access. I had already attempted to leave the church once, only to discover the invisible barrier blocking me. Who invented these ghostly rules, I didn't know, but they were there and they were damned limiting.

The classrooms all looked just as I remembered: lots of shelving and lots of religious-themed posters. Maybe even the *same* posters back from my school days. GOD IS GREAT. JESUS IS THE REASON FOR THE SEASON.

The teachers, granted, were younger and far cuter than I remembered.

Sometimes, as I drifted in and out of the various classrooms, students would turn and look at me—then usually quickly look away. Young mediums, all of them. The world is full of such mediums; most just won't admit to their abilities.

Now, as I drifted through the back wall of a third-grade classroom, a redheaded kid with braces and a thick neck snapped his head around and looked directly at me, then promptly turned bone white. Then again, maybe he was already bone white. Hard to tell with redheads.

Unfortunately for him, I was in a strange and bitter mood, and as I passed him, I said, "Boo."

He slammed his eyes shut. The kid was a powerful medium in the making, whether he wanted to be or not. Probably not, since he was now making the sign of the cross and might have just wet himself.

Scaring little boys is not the way to go to heaven, I thought.

I continued drifting down the aisle toward the head of the class, where the teacher was droning on about the Spanish colonies of yesteryear. On the wall just behind her were various class portraits spanning many decades.

The class portraits gave me an idea. A very good idea.

Now, just don't forget it!

* * *

I whipped down a hallway, made a sharp right, and found myself in the school's administration office, which was being manned by a young, serious-looking woman in her early twenties.

The sign on her desk read VISITORS, SIGN IN.

I was tempted to write *James the Ghost*.

Instead, I drifted past her and down a narrow hallway lined with doors on either side. I peeked into all of them, whether they were open or not, and in the very last room, I finally found what I was searching for.

It was the copy room, and on the wide shelf above the workstation was a very long row of school yearbooks.

25

Ghosts are energy.

I understand this now, although I didn't before. And when I say "before," I mean back when I was living. Hell, back when I was living, I didn't even believe in ghosts, let alone that someday I would actually *be* one. Then again, maybe I wasn't a ghost. Maybe all this was one long, bad dream. A very, very bad dream.

Or maybe this is hell, I thought.

At that moment, a very large, balding man stepped into the copy room. He flicked on the light switch and ignored me completely and opened the copy machine's lid. He punched in the number 30 and proceeded to run off thirty copies of what appeared to be a drawing of a pizza.

Aww, fractions.

While the copy machine chugged away, he shivered and rubbed his arms and looked around absently—and perhaps a little uneasily. His very weak sixth sense was picking up on me.

When his copies were finished, he turned to leave, but then paused in the doorway. The fine hairs on the back of his neck, I saw, were standing on end. He slowly, slowly turned around—and appeared to look directly at me.

Did he see me? I didn't know. I doubted it. A small part of his brain knew I was there, but could he trust that part of his brain?

Most people didn't. He continued staring at me. I stared back at him. Somewhere down the hallway, a phone rang. Someone answered it. He blinked first, shivered once, and then got the hell out of Dodge—or at least the hell out of the copy room.

When he was gone, I went to work.

* * *

As a ghost, I could draw energy from most anywhere: from the air, from the sun, from the living—and even from electronics.

Especially from electronics.

Ghosts and electronics were made for each other, which was why lights in a house often flickered during a haunting. Ghosts, you see, used the electricity that fed the lights as an energy source to materialize.

And so now, with the help of the copy machine, I began to materialize. And as I did so, the lights from its display panel flickered wildly, and the whole thing sort of groaned, like something old and dying.

I felt myself taking shape. First, my torso formed; then, in a sort of rippling wave of solidity, my arms and legs and fingers and toes appeared. I turned my hand over, watching it congeal before my eyes, opening and closing my fingers, making a fist. I sucked more energy from the machine, from the air, from anywhere and everywhere I could find it. Galvanized and crackling with life, I imagined this was how Frankenstein's monster felt when that lightning storm struck.

Where's Igor when you need him?

Solid and fully formed and feeling more alive than I had in a long, long time, I was just about to get to work when the secretary appeared in the doorway.

77

* * *

Shit.

Head down and holding a piece of paper she no doubt intended to copy, she absently reached for the light switch—and then paused midreach.

Her head snapped up and she gasped. How she didn't scream, I don't know. She put a hand over her chest and calmed herself.

"Oh, my God, you scared me. I didn't think anyone was in here."

I just smiled and nodded—and prayed she wouldn't continue reaching for the light switch. My bullet wounds would have been hard to miss in this form.

"Um, I'll come back," she said, backing away. "Do you need any light?"

I shook my head, and she stared at me for another moment, then turned and hustled off.

I knew I didn't have much time. Ghost or no ghost, a strange man standing alone in the copy room—with the lights out, no less—would warrant an investigation.

I moved quickly over to the shelf filled with yearbooks.

I figured the killer, Eli, was in his late twenties. If so, that would have put him in high school about ten years ago. Which, if my math was right, would have made him about eight years younger than I was.

So I started pulling down yearbooks that corresponded with those dates. I pulled out four yearbooks and opened the cover to the first—and briefly reveled in my solidity. I was nearly 100 percent congealed, and I felt almost human. Well, human enough to turn the pages of the book, which I did now, flipping rapidly to the high school portraits, scanning faces, looking for the killer.

The church's private school was not a big one, so I was able to go through the high school students rather quickly. Nothing in the first yearbook. I opened the second, repeating the process of scanning faces. Nothing there, either. I pushed it off to the side, opened the third. When that proved fruitless, I went for the fourth. I had just opened it, had just happened across the high school football team photo, when I heard voices coming down the hallway.

They were coming.

Which was a damn shame, since I had just spotted Eli.

26

There were times—rare times, granted—when I was thankful for being a ghost. This was one of them.

As the footsteps and voices drew nearer, I stepped away from the copy machine and, with my source of energy now gone, immediately began to evaporate. Just as I had risen up off the floor, two men, trailed by the secretary, entered the copy room.

One of them immediately flicked on the light, but by that time, I was already hovering near the ceiling and, should they have looked up, would have appeared only as a nearly invisible, misty sheen. And even the mist was fading quickly. Soon I would be gone altogether.

Gone, but not forgotten.

Both men were wearing blue jeans and T-shirts. Teachers, perhaps. Or maybe coaches. Hard to tell, since teachers dressed so casually nowadays. The secretary stepped cautiously into the room between the two men. She looked completely flabbergasted.

"He was just here," she said. "Standing in the dark, doing nothing."

"Who was he?" one of the guys asked.

"I don't know."

"What did he look like?" asked the other.

"Tall. Hair sort of mussed. Then again, he was in the dark."

"What was he doing?" asked the first guy.

"Like I said, nothing. Just standing there. Looking creepy as heck. I've been watching the door from my desk ever since. No one left."

"Did he say anything?"

"No."

The men looked at each other. One raised an eyebrow. The secretary saw the gesture and immediately turned on him.

"Look, I'm not making this up, Rick," she said.

"I didn't say you were."

She moved deeper into the room, pointed to the open yearbooks. "Look. These were not like this before."

"He was looking at yearbooks in the dark?" Rick asked, incredulous.

"I don't know. Maybe—"

"Sharon—"

"Don't *Sharon* me."

The men exchanged looks again, this one much more patronizing. Luckily, Sharon didn't see this. Instead, she was looking down at her arms, the flesh of which had dimpled into goose bumps.

"Why is this room so darn cold? It's usually stifling in here." She rubbed her arms and shoulders, then felt the air around her. She reached up. "The cold, it's coming from up here." Her hand passed through my groin. "It's coming from here. It's, like, twenty degrees cooler here."

The men looked at each other again; cold spots apparently didn't excite them.

"Sharon," said Rick evenly, carefully, "no one saw a man come in here, and no one saw a man leave. Just like—"

"Just like what?" she asked, spinning around. Sharon was a young girl, perhaps in college. She would have been cute if she weren't so pissed off. "Just like the little boy I see in the nave?"

"Yes," said the other guy. "The boy you *claim* to see."

"He's there, Jules. And I'm not the only one who sees him." Her voice rose an octave or two.

He held up his hands. "Okay, okay. We'll take a walk around campus, see if we can find anyone," said Jules. "Does that make you feel better?"

She nodded, appeased, but still didn't like it. I felt a little sorry for her. The men exited, and she was left standing there alone, looking up at the ceiling. Looking up at me. She knew I was there. Or a part of her did.

"Whoever you are," she said, "I command you to leave here, in the name of Jesus Christ."

Where was I supposed to go? I didn't know, but I knew when I wasn't wanted, so I drifted through the wall, out into the hallway, and exited the administrative offices.

* * *

I waited until the dead of night to return to the copy room.

Jacob had followed me halfway there but had gotten distracted by some new artwork tacked onto the hallway bulletin board. He was, after all, just a kid. How old, exactly, I didn't know, but I would guess under ten, maybe seven or eight.

The offices were, of course, dark and empty. The copy machine itself was in some sort of hibernation mode. So I gathered as much energy as I could, no doubt chilling the air around me, and pressed the activation button on the machine. The copier immediately whirred on. A few minutes later, when it was fully charged, I drew enough energy from it to pull down the same yearbook I had seen Eli in.

I opened it and went looking for the same football team shot. I found the photo again in the athletics section, and there he was, a clean-cut kid with a smirk on his face, his wide shoulder pads making him appear much bigger and tougher than he really was. I quickly found his corresponding name in the caption below the picture.

Eli Myrth.

I read it again and again. The name of my killer. The name of my piano teacher's killer.

And that's when it hit me. I remembered Eli Myrth.

Lord help me, I remembered.

I need that wallet.

27

I dashed out of the copy room, through the administration offices, flashed down a hallway.

I made an impossible ninety-degree turn at what would have been breakneck speed. Except, of course, I didn't have a neck to break. I passed the dead boy. He was skipping in and out of a wall covered with photos of a recent school play, humming to himself.

The boy…

Lord, help me.

The double doors to the nave were closed. No problem. I lowered my head, blasted through.

The church, as usual, was dark and empty and eerie as hell. I whipped down the main aisle, up the platform, and into the side storage room off stage left.

The room was pitch-dark. I didn't need much light, but I did need some, so I gathered my energy and used it all to flick on the light switch. Once done, I headed over to the box where Eli Myrth had hidden the wallet weeks earlier.

Thankfully, the wallet was still there, wedged deep within a tangle of black cables.

I tried to gather my energy enough to lift the wallet, but my thoughts were scattered, laced with images of Jacob falling to his death.

Horrible, horrible images.

Earlier, Jacob's perspective had been as he fell, looking up at the shocked and horrified faces of the boys who had dropped him.

My perspective—my *new* perspective—was from above, watching in horror as the boy began to slip from my grasp, realizing with horror that something very bad was about to happen.

Very, very bad.

The boy reaches up, helplessly.

But it's too late, and now he's falling, falling…

* * *

We just meant to scare him.

I tried to calm down. Tried to focus my thoughts. No good. I paced the small area of the storage room, shook my hands. If I could have taken a deep breath, I would have.

We just meant to scare him.

I needed that wallet. I needed to know what was inside, although I could already guess. I forced myself to calm down, to slow down. Back at the cardboard box, I gathered my energy as best I could and plucked the wallet out from within. It dropped to the floor, flopped open.

I hovered over the wallet, wondering if I really wanted to know what was inside. Yes, I did. Very much so. It was truly a matter of life and death.

Well, *after*life and death.

I leaned down over the wallet, then removed two items from their respective slots. The first was a Subway lunch card. Four holes had been punched—just six away from a free sub. The other was a student ID card. The student in the picture had a minor acne problem, but nothing that time wouldn't eventually clear up.

He was grinning and happy, a spark in his eye. The spark would later leave with the weight of guilt. Eternal guilt.

The name on the card was mine, of course.

James Blakely.

28

Pauline and I were kneeling together in the front pew.

She had come to light a prayer candle to save the souls of those languishing in purgatory—that, and to see how the hell I was doing. Personally, I think she and I were connected somehow. And my own internal anguish had registered on her psychic radar. Or not. Maybe she really did miss me after just a few days.

Also, I wasn't so much kneeling as floating next to her in a kneeling sort of way. She lit another candle, mumbled something that I couldn't hear.

"Say a little prayer for me, too," I said.

"Already did."

"What did God say?"

"He'll get back to me."

"It figures."

We weren't alone in the nave. Jacob was nearby, miming playing the piano onstage with big, exaggerated movements that he might have learned from various Bugs Bunny cartoons. Every now and then, he actually struck a real key and a real note erupted from the piano, and the handful of worshippers would gasp and look up and cross themselves immediately. Pauline would just giggle next to me. Jacob himself seemed completely oblivious to the fact that he was sometimes scaring the hell out of the parishioners. Instead, he would often stop his pseudoplaying and sob uncontrollably, his little shoulders shaking violently, the sound of his weeping reaching my ears—and Pauline's ears—quite easily.

"The boy misses his music teacher," said Pauline.

"Yes."

"And he misses something else."

I looked over at her. Damn, she was perceptive.

"Yes," I said. "I imagine he does."

"He had a twin brother," she said.

"Yes, he did."

Between my own telltale thoughts and the boy's erratic memories, I was willing to bet Pauline knew most of what was going on already.

I said nothing. In death, events in my past had mostly stayed forgotten, unless I was reminded of them. Being here, in this church, I was reminded of them. Powerfully. And ever since I had found the wallet, memories of Jacob's death had been flooding back all day. Haunting, horrible memories. And with them returned the terrible feelings of guilt.

I didn't mean to drop him, I thought.

I was just going to scare him into telling me where my wallet was.

"You killed that little boy," said Pauline. Despite herself, despite our friendship and her love for me, there was a note of accusation in her voice.

I nodded. I could feel the weight of Pauline's stare on me.

"Yes," I said. "I and one other."

"Tell me what happened."

I did. As best as I could remember, I told her how someone had spotted Jacob going through my backpack, stealing my wallet. Because we were in a K–12 private school, we sometimes mixed with the younger kids. Jacob, if my sketchy memory was correct, had been about eight at the time. I had been sixteen, just beginning my junior year of high school.

I had grabbed a friend of mine, a friend whose name I could not recall at the moment. Together, he and I found Jacob in one of the bathrooms. We told him that the piano teacher wanted to see him, and followed him into the empty nave. Once inside, we grabbed the boy and dragged him, kicking and screaming, up a flight of stairs to the rafters above the sanctuary. Rafters meant only for the lighting guys—not for cruel teenage boys.

We hung Jacob over the railing. Demanded he tell us where my wallet was. The kid was hysterical. Didn't know where the wallet was—claimed he didn't know what we were talking about. *But he was lying! I knew it!* He had been caught red-handed by someone I trusted. We were furious. Well, I was furious. My friend was just caught up in the moment.

So I hung him farther out over the railing, demanded that he tell me where my wallet was…

And then it happened.

I couldn't believe it at first. One moment he was in my hands, struggling, fighting, scared out of his mind. The next he was falling through the air, reaching up for us, eyes wide and terrified. I lunged forward, reached out for him, but he was gone.

Gone.

And if he had landed on the carpeted stage, he would have probably suffered only a broken leg or two. Instead, he hit the sharp corner of the heavy altar, and his head burst open, spraying blood and brain matter across the sanctuary. He jerked once, twice, and then lay still.

I watched him die from the rafters.

* * *

Pauline was silent, digesting.

Jacob's death was a memory I had relived a million times. To some degree, my own death had been a welcome relief, for then the memories of the falling boy had abated—at least for a few years.

Now they were back again.

A million and one times, I had watched Jacob fall; a million and one times, I had watched his head explode, saw the blood, his brains...saw it all again.

And again.

I looked up toward the rafters now.

And it had all happened right here, in this place. I glanced to my right. And there he was now, the dead boy, silently playing the piano, his head eternally broken open.

All because of me.

Sweet, sweet Jesus. What have I done?

"Don't be so hard on yourself, James," said Pauline. "I have a feeling you've beaten yourself up enough over this."

I didn't say anything. Didn't know what to say. Beating myself up over this was a natural pastime for me. Hell, I had killed a kid. I deserved to beat myself up over this, right?

"No," said Pauline. "You need to forgive yourself."

"No," I said. "I need *him* to forgive *me.*"

We both looked at the boy. Jacob was flamboyantly playing the piano in a ghostly imitation of Liberace.

Pauline dipped deeper into my thoughts. "But that's not the worst of it, is it?" she asked.

"No," I said. Pain coursed through me. So real and powerful that I wanted to sink down into the floor and keep on sinking forever.

"Jacob didn't steal your wallet, did he?" she said.

"No," I said, looking away. "It was his twin brother, Eli."

29

"The same twin who later killed you?"

"Yes."

"The same twin who killed the music teacher? Her name, by the way, was Mrs. Randolph."

Ah. The name resonated deep within me. Pauline continued probing my mind. She was a hell of a prober.

"I'll take that as a compliment," she said. "I think. Anyway, why did Eli wait so long to come after you?"

"I don't know," I said. "Does it matter?"

"Probably not, but I'll check into some things."

"Check how?" I asked.

"With a private investigator I know. We've worked on some cases together."

"You work with a private investigator?" I asked.

"Sometimes. Hey, psychic detectives are all the rage these days. I happen to provide an invaluable service."

"Okay, fine," I said. "See what you can find out, but I don't think it really matters, does it?"

I thought about what I had just said, and realized my error.

Pauline picked up on my thoughts, too. "Exactly," she said. "This friend of yours who helped you haul Jacob up to the rafters..."

"Is in some serious danger," I finished.

"Or already dead," she said. "Do you remember his name?"

"No."

"I'll have my detective friend check everything out in one fell swoop. I'll be back when I have something."

We were silent. The church was active. Worshippers came and went. The boy continued miming playing the piano. Luckily, he had stopped inadvertently hitting the keys. Which was just as well. Wouldn't want the church to get a reputation for being haunted or anything.

"Do you hate Eli for killing you?" Pauline asked suddenly.

A good question.

"No," I said, surprising even myself. "At least, I don't think I do. A part of me thinks I deserved to die. After all, I had taken so much away from him."

"And now he has taken so much away from you."

I thought about my daughter. I hated that she was going to grow up without her daddy. I also hated that I hadn't been given a chance to make my life right, to correct my mistakes, to guarantee my entry into heaven.

Pauline, of course, was reading my thoughts. "Maybe there is no guarantee, James."

"What do you mean?"

"I mean, maybe sooner or later it's time to roll the dice."

"Excuse me, but I'd rather not roll the dice with my eternal soul, thank you. I would rather stay here and do what I'm doing than burn in hell forever."

"Fine. And what if I told you there was no hell, James? And, for that matter, no heaven, either?"

"I would say you were full of shit."

"What if I told you that when you die, you go somewhere else? Another plane of existence, a spirit world filled with family and friends and love?"

"I would say prove it."

"Some things have to be taken on faith, James."

"So you say," I said.

30

It was late, and Jacob and I were alone in the cathedral.

The kid had wandered up to the very rafters where he had fallen. Or, more accurately, where I had *dropped* him. He was often drawn to that spot, and I wondered if he even knew *why* he was. Maybe, maybe not. Either way, his memory was spotty at best, and the details of his own death were mostly lost to him. *Mercifully.*

Someday soon I was going to have to come clean with him, to admit to him what I had done. And that was going to be a very, very difficult day.

I was sitting in a pew, near the main aisle, in a pool of moonlight that shone down through the stained-glass windows above. Outside, there must have been a small wind blowing. The crooked shadows of skeletal branches waved across the floor and pews like somebody beckoning somebody, and as I sat there alone, gazing at nothing and everything, one shadow in particular seemed to come alive in the far corner of the room. It was high up, near the ceiling. First, it appeared as a sort of inkblot, separating from the deeper shadows of the ceiling. Then it moved sideways across the ceiling, developing arms and legs as it went. Many arms and legs. And many eyes. It paused once along the ceiling and turned toward me.

Apparently, I wasn't alone.

* * *

The shadow was, in fact, *three* shadows. They appeared vaguely humanoid, with three sets of reddish eyes and many spiderlike limbs. They also appeared to be moving as one, with calculated, coordinated movements. Perhaps I should have been scared. Perhaps I should have fled the nave in terror.

But I didn't. What could they do? Kill me again?

With Jacob still high in the rafters, lost in his scattered thoughts, the three shadows continued creeping sideways along the wall. Their glowing eyes, I was certain, were trained on me. Whoever—or whatever—they were, I seemed to have their undivided attention.

Lucky me.

As they got closer, scuttling unusually along the wall like some great black insect, I was able to reach out and dip into their minds and sense who—or *what*—they were.

I immediately sensed great confusion and loss and fear and pain. So much pain. And flashing, distorted, murky, incomprehensible memories. Human memories.

They were human. Or *were* human.

What they were now, I did not know. Shadows of their former selves. Memories of their former selves, reduced now to nonsensical creatures who were completely out of their minds, having lost all memory of who they were or why they were even in the church…

No, that isn't right.

I did sense a purpose. A single, undivided purpose that seemed somehow woven throughout their mostly fragmented memories. I looked up at the painting on the wall in front of me. The purpose had something to do with it—but what that purpose was, I did not know.

The entities crept closer.

They seemed two-dimensional, as if there were no essence to them, no depth. True shadows. Shades. They continued along the wall to my left, crawling just beneath the stained-glass windows. The bright moonlight seemed lost on them, swallowed by them.

Living black holes.

This will be you someday, I suddenly thought. *Losing your mind, your memory, the very essence of who you are. Forever.*

With that pleasant thought in mind, the three entities, which had worked their way along the wall directly across from me, now stopped. They seemed to be communicating with one another. Shortly, they came to some sort of an agreement, and as they did so, something unexpected happened.

Like rotting wallpaper, they peeled away from the wall and then slowly drifted out over the pews.

A demon kite, I thought, looking up at the specters drifting over me like a Macy's Thanksgiving Day Parade float from hell.

Now closer, I was able to dip deeper into their lost minds. And what I found there were many distorted, disturbing, chaotic images: flashes of gunfire, swirling monks' robes, the sneering of cruel thieves, unimaginable torture. Again, all centered on the massive oil painting hanging on the far wall.

"Indeed, James," said a female voice suddenly to my right, startling me. "They guard the painting. And they do so quite well, don't you think?"

I had been so caught up watching the steady approach of the three entities that I had completely missed the woman who had materialized onstage. She was, of course, the beautiful woman from my apartment complex, the beautiful woman whom I had no memory of. From across the cathedral, she smiled at me, then looked up. I followed her gaze. There, the three shadows were now suspended nearly directly above me. Creepy as hell, if you ask me.

"They were monks once," she said, her melodic voice filling my head. "More significant, they were brothers, and all three were tortured and murdered here in this very church."

I frowned. "But if they were monks, then why are they not in heaven?"

"They made a pact, James. A pact in life that they now carry into death."

"A pact?"

"To protect the painting you see on the wall above me."

Yes, the painting. It was a massive portrait of the Mount of Olives, depicting Christ's betrayal and arrest prior to his crucifixion. The same painting Eli had lusted after—and run in terror from.

"You see, there had been a *fourth* brother," she said.

I nodded with sudden clarity. "The artist who painted it."

"Indeed," she said, stepping off the stage. "The painting was commissioned by the Catholic Church and was to be brought to the New World. But the fourth brother, the artist, died of the plague upon its completion, and the remaining three brothers took it upon themselves to transport it safely. The painting eventually found its way here, to this church, where both the painting and brothers took up residence."

"Until the thieves came," I said.

She nodded. "Banditos. They were after the painting, among other things. But the brothers, given advance warning of their arrival, had safely hidden it. The banditos were not happy. Each brother was systematically tortured and killed, but the painting remained safely hidden. Centuries later, it was discovered in the bowels of the church's basement, and now, as you can see, it hangs prominently."

I looked directly up. "And still they watch over it."

"Vigilantly," said the woman. "And forsaking all of heaven to do so."

She now stood in the aisle before me. I rose to my feet and stared into those heartbreakingly familiar almond-shaped eyes. I knew those eyes. I knew that face. I knew those lips. Intimately. But I had no memory of her. Nothing.

"Who are you?" I asked.

She took my hand, and for the first time in a long, long time, I felt warmth. I also felt love. Deep, fathomless love. As she held my gaze, images appeared in my mind. Beautiful, sweet, loving images of the two of us together, throughout time and space, born and reborn throughout many lifetimes, dozens of lifetimes. Hundreds of lifetimes. The images came fast and crazily, until at last they finally slowed and stopped. Now two words appeared in my thoughts, pulsating, alive with meaning: *soul mates*.

This was followed by a final image. One of a beautiful college student with long blonde hair, an impish smile, and almond-shaped eyes. A student who had been killed instantly in a car accident that had left me reeling for many, many years, until I eventually met my future wife.

"You're her!" I said, thunderstruck, as a wave of dizziness and disorientation threatened to overwhelm me. Had I been alive, I would have needed to sit. Had I been alive, I would, of course, not have been holding her hands.

She squeezed mine even tighter. "Yes, James."

"And we've been reincarnated together?" I asked, remembering the images. "Throughout all eternity?"

"Yes, James."

I sensed the truth behind her words, behind her images, but I was troubled. Deeply, deeply troubled. How could I reincarnate if I was given but one chance at life, one chance to make things right? This was how I was raised to believe. This was what the church taught.

I released her hands. "I don't believe you."

"Your belief is everything, James."

"I think you're the Devil," I said, "here to tempt me."

And even as I spoke those words, I knew them to be untrue. How could anyone love me the way she loved me now and be the Devil? Could the Devil even love?

She continued watching me; I continued feeling her love.

Behind her, the three brothers dropped from the ceiling and, as if they had forgotten the use of their legs, crawled along the center aisle on hands and feet as their knees and elbows stuck out at odd angles. As they approached behind her, they could have easily been demons. *Her* demons. She ignored them and continued staring at me steadily. I found them to be distracting as hell.

I forced myself to look into her eyes. "I can't believe you," I said. "I'm sorry."

"Someday you will, James." And with that, she began fading before my eyes. And when she had disappeared altogether, the three red-eyed beings immediately retreated down the center aisle and scuttled up the far wall and disappeared into the darkest shadows of the deepest part of the ceiling.

But I knew they were up there.

Watching.

31

Days passed, maybe even weeks.

I haunted the old church, the school of my youth, location of so much death and destruction. Often, I sat in on classroom lectures, learning much about history and science and social studies. All of which I forgot instantly. Just like back when I was in school. *Some things never change.*

My friends now were the parishioners and the teachers and the students and the workers. Except, they didn't know I was their friend. Mostly, my companions were Jacob and the three red-eyed beings that watched over the massive painting with unsettling single-mindedness. But not always. Sometimes they watched me, too, doing so with a unique oneness. Sometimes the three wraiths would come down from the ceiling and swarm around me like curious red-eyed demon cats. But they weren't evil, and if they were, I certainly didn't sense it.

Often, I had to remind myself of who I was and why I was here. And sometimes I couldn't even do that. Whole days would pass until I finally remembered who I was, and then it would all come flooding back to me—all of it, all over again, reliving everything and everyone. Jacob's death, my murder, Mrs. Randolph's murder. And I would weep for my dead body, my fatherless girl, and my own lost soul.

But I would weep hardest for taking the life of the young boy.

Once or twice, when I had lost all sense of who I was, I found myself creeping along the ceiling with the three entities. They accepted me as one of their own, and I found their presence oddly comforting. I found their communal thoughts a blessing, their collective will attractive. They referred to themselves as The One, and I liked that. We were The One.

That is, until I would remember who I was. Then I would peel away from the trio. But each time, it was harder and harder to leave them. There is peace in numbers. I needed peace.

Mostly, I haunted the classrooms and naves and back offices and forgotten rooms. Sometimes I remembered my daughter, but mostly I didn't. Sometimes I remembered my wife, but that, too, was becoming a rarity. Sometimes I would see a beautiful young woman watching me from the shadows, glowing in her own bright light, and I would wonder who she was.

* * *

I knew the day would come when I would tell the boy my identity. That I was, in fact, his killer.

I also knew that how I came to be here at this church, at this time, with him, wasn't a coincidence. Then again, maybe it was. But I doubted it. Something bigger was going on here, some grand reconciliation that I didn't entirely comprehend. Too much of this seemed preordained. Too much of this seemed to have the touch of something greater going on.

Or not. We would see.

Still, the time did not seem right to tell Jacob.

Soon, I thought. *Very soon.*

* * *

Pauline checked in on me every now and then.

On this day, as we sat together in the front pew, she informed me that my memory was disappearing at a much faster rate because I was not naturally grounded to the church, that my memory would keep disappearing until I was nothing more than one of the red-eyed entities watching over the painting. I didn't tell her that I was, in fact, already becoming like them, but I think she sensed it anyway.

I asked her again why I was here and what had happened to me, and with great patience, she told me again. I sensed she had told me this dozens and dozens of times before. Perhaps hundreds. I didn't know.

As we sat there, Pauline took my hand and told me I needed to leave this place before I lost all sense of who I was. I told her I needed to be here until some resolution came, no matter how difficult the road ahead may be. She had nodded and was about to leave when I put a hand on her forearm. Or tried to. Mostly, my hand just passed through her. As sensitive as she was, she was aware of the gesture, and paused.

"Wait," I said. "How long have I been here?"

"Two months."

"How's my daughter?"

"I don't know, but I'm sure she's fine."

"I miss her," I said.

She smiled at me sadly and told me she would be back. I watched her go, and as she exited, the red-eyed beings crawled down from the ceiling and swarmed around me.

Just one big happy family.

32

I was sitting with Jacob in an empty classroom.

It was late evening and school was out and the teachers had all long since gone home. Only a handful of spooked maintenance workers remained. I wondered what had gotten them so spooked.

Jacob and I didn't talk much these days. I just couldn't find it within me to ask about his family, especially his brother. He seemed content with silence. I suspected he was very used to silence after so many years haunting the church alone.

We were sitting in a fifth-grade classroom, surrounded by surprisingly competent student artwork. I spilled out of the small desk I was squeezed in, although Jacob sat comfortably within his. Our sitting, of course, was just an illusion. In reality, we simply contorted our ethereal bodies in a parody of sitting, and if you looked closely enough, we were both rising and falling gently on the ghostly tides of this nether dimension we occupied.

Jacob was humming a song, a Beatles song, I think—"I Want to Hold Your Hand." But he was butchering it badly, having forgotten the words and most of the basic tune.

I thought about my desire to save my own soul. Was I making any progress? I didn't know. I had found Mrs. Randolph's killer, sure, but her killer had turned out to be *my* killer. And now *our* killer was the twin brother of the boy I had killed so many years ago.

Coincidence?

I doubted it. There was too much going on here. What it was, I didn't know.

And as Jacob continued butchering the Beatles song and I continued contemplating my eternal fate, a television production crew arrived at the church. And according to all their shirts and equipment and gear, they were here to film something called *Ghost Detectives*.

Great.

33

The TV crew, making a hell of a racket, set up shop in one of the third-grade classrooms.

Loud enough to wake the dead.

Jacob and I were sitting together in the far corner of the classroom, minus our dunce caps, watching as the film crew quickly and efficiently set up their equipment. Most of the workers were wearing black T-shirts with green lettering. The green lettering said, GHOST DETECTIVES.

I've lived in LA most of my adult life. At least, I'm pretty sure I have. I do have a vague memory of living in Phoenix for a brief period, but that memory was elusive at best and I didn't put a whole lot of stock into it. Hell, lately I didn't put a whole lot of stock into *any* of my memories.

Anyway, growing up here in LA, especially near Hollywood, one gets used to seeing such film crews, and the glamour of it all wears off real quick. But this situation was different, and I was admittedly excited.

"What are they doing?" Jacob asked next to me.

"They're filming a television show," I said.

"About what?"

"Us, I think."

He looked up at me, his mouth forming a perfect oval of surprise. "Us? But why?"

"Because we're special," I said. *Because we're ghosts*, I didn't add.

"But they can't see us," said Jacob. "*Nobody* can see us."

I watched the crew scurry about, testing lights and cameras and clip-on microphones. As they did so, another group stepped into the room—three guys and a girl—all wearing the same *Ghost Detectives* T-shirts. But these four felt different to me. Waves of arrogant self-importance radiated from them.

Ah, the stars are here, I thought.

Immediately, one of them raised a fit. Apparently, someone was supposed to have a coffee ready for him. He was a tall guy with a shiny ponytail, held in place by three evenly spaced rubber bands. An assistant scurried off and returned shortly with a steaming cup of Starbucks. The man received it without a thank-you and promptly sent the assistant, almost in tears now, off to another task. I looked over at the boy.

"Perhaps we should *let* them see us," I said.

"I don't understand," said Jacob.

I smiled at him. "Do you want to have some fun? Play a game with them?"

He thought about that. I think the concept of fun and games was almost lost on him. I planted an image of hide-and-seek in his mind, and his eyes lit up.

"Yes!" he said, clapping. "Yes, let's have some fun!"

34

I recognized the school secretary there, too, conferring with a small group of the *Ghost Detectives* directors and producers.

Had she arranged all of this? I suspected so. Ghost sightings, undoubtedly, had been on the rise in the church and school since my arrival. And perhaps my presence here had prompted more activity from Jacob as well.

Standing next to the secretary was the school principal, a tall, distinguished-looking lady drinking her own Starbucks coffee and looking very concerned—no doubt wondering what the hell she had agreed to.

I would have been concerned, too.

Interestingly, there were no mediums in the group. I would have thought ghost detecting involved a good medium, but what the hell did I know? I was just a spook. Anyway, with no medium in the group, I was able to flit among them sight unseen, with Jacob trailing behind like a ghostly duckling.

I worked my way over to the corner of the room, near the teacher's desk, where the quartet of stars had isolated themselves away from the rest of the crew. The guy with the ponytail was adamantly arguing his point that he should investigate the nave. Turned out they all wanted to investigate the parish; in particular, they all appeared to want a close-up shot with a bloody Jesus

Christ hanging over their shoulder. Ponytail smugly won out in the end by pulling rank. It seemed to me that the show was more about getting close-ups of its stars than about hunting ghosts. Big surprise.

Well, they were about to get a surprise. Perhaps the surprise of their lives.

Showtime.

35

It was midnight. The witching hour. Or, in this case, the *haunting hour*.

With cameras rolling, the secretary gave the crew—along with Jacob and me—a tour of the brightly lit school and cathedral. She gave a rundown of the many unexplainable sights and sounds the parishioners and students and teachers had all seen or heard, and by the end of the tour, I was damn well convinced the place was haunted.

Once the tour was done, the cast and crew created a sort of storyboard for how they wanted the show to flow. The plan was basic: the teams would split in two, with one group filming primarily in the cathedral and the other in the school and administrative offices. The teams might overlap, depending on what evidence was discovered or whether personal experiences needed to be confirmed or validated. Most of the ghost-hunting equipment would be used in the cathedral, since it was not only the most visually stunning room, but where most of the unexplainable sightings had occurred. The team investigating the administrative offices, where I had been spotted, and adjacent school and classrooms, where Jacob did most of his haunting, would be given limited equipment. Ponytail looked smug. He would be getting most of the camera time this episode, and it obviously pleased him.

At any rate, I approved of the game plan. Made sense to me. Of course, no one asked me.

And because I could, as the crew was preparing to split for this evening's investigation, I leaned over and kissed the female star square on the lips.

Her eyes widened immediately. "Did someone just turn on the AC?" she asked.

"I don't think so. Why?" asked the young director.

"I just got a cold blast of air in my face."

That seemed to get everyone's attention. The director came over and felt the air around her. I had stepped off to the side and watched the proceedings with some interest, and maybe a little humor. He had some of the others feel the air around her, then proclaimed, rather dramatically, that there was no cold breeze coming from anywhere.

"But look at my arm," she said, pushing up her sleeve.

They all did. So did I. Her forearm, I saw, was covered in gooseflesh. The young director, no dummy, got a camera over to her ASAP. And as they filmed both of her arms, I walked straight through the director himself.

He convulsed and nearly doubled over. "Sweet Jesus! Something just went right through me." He shoved up his own sleeve. "Look."

We all looked. It, too, was covered in goose bumps. The same cameraman took some footage of the director's mottled skin as well.

Ah, TV at its best.

A ripple of excitement was now spreading through the crew. I heard the murmurings: perhaps they were going to have a good show, after all.

Little did they know...

With the whole crew buzzing in anticipation, the investigation began. Cameras began rolling. Ponytail, who appeared to be the *Ghost Detectives* leader, looked each of his investigators directly in the eye and intoned ominously, "Let's go black."

Apparently, that meant to kill the lights. Which they all did. Last time I checked, ghosts didn't stop existing or *start* existing because of the absence, or presence, of light. Hell, we derive much of our energy from lights—especially the light of the sun, which we sort of feed off of. So killing the lights was counterproductive, although it made for better TV. Then again, no one asked me. Typical.

As one team headed for the administrative office, Ponytail and a good-looking kid split off toward the cathedral, trailed by two cameramen.

And, of course, two ghosts.

36

Ponytail, who had the annoying habit of dramatically flipping his namesake over a shoulder whenever he turned his head, was extremely thin and sinewy and had skin so orange it looked nearly radioactive. The color probably looked good on camera, even if it scared small children in line at Baskin-Robbins.

Admittedly, I didn't like him; in fact, I might have irrationally hated him.

Hey, ghosts are allowed to be irrational.

The other guy was okay. He was younger, humbler, and better looking. He also seemed to take this ghost-hunting business a little more seriously. He was also mildly sensitive, the closest thing they had to a medium. Every now and then, his eyes would drift over in my direction, linger, and then look away. He knew *something* was there, but he didn't know what, and he also didn't know if he could fully trust his extrasensory perceptions.

In this case, yes, he could very much trust them.

With Jacob already looking bored, I followed the two ghost detectives and their cameramen into the nave. And since nobody held the doors open for Jacob and me, we simply walked through them.

Once inside the main chapel, the cameramen swept their powerful lights over the pews and stage and podium. In the dark, everything looked appropriately creepy.

The two detectives separated to cover more of the chapel. Ponytail and his cameraman headed up to the stage, while the younger guy and his cameraman headed toward the rear pews.

I followed Ponytail.

Taking an active interest in the proceedings, the red-eyed beings crept out of the shadows of the ceiling and stopped about a quarter of the way down the wall. Lord help anyone who touched that painting. Anyway, unless you knew what you were looking for, they appeared to be nothing more than shadows cast by the outside tree.

Ponytail was now standing directly beneath the statue of Jesus Christ. "Let's get some shots of me standing here."

The cameraman obliged, dropping to a knee and angling his camera in such a way that he got both Ponytail and Christ in the same shot. The former struck a very intrepid pose as he slowly surveyed the dangerously haunted inner sanctuary. Ponytail next walked over to the piano and, with the cameraman trailing behind, turned and looked somberly into the lens.

"Over the years," he whispered with pseudoreverence, sliding his fingers over the closed piano keyboard cover, "there have been many reports of this piano mysteriously playing itself." He paused and flipped his thick ponytail from his right shoulder to his left, a completely unnecessary move. He went on. "And, in a surprising twist, the school's music teacher was found murdered on this same piano just a few months ago."

As he glided his hand slowly over the closed lid, I drew some energy from the camera light—which caused it to flicker—and reached down through the closed wooden lid and struck a key.

A minor key, I think.

The sound echoed through the sanctuary, and Ponytail nearly did a backflip. He jumped about a foot or two off the ground and landed on his cameraman. Both landed in a heap.

When they had untangled, the cameraman, who looked a little pissed, said, "What the hell happened?"

"Something pressed the key down!" said Ponytail excitedly.

"You mean, *you* pressed the key," said the cameraman.

Ponytail spun on him. "How the fuck could I press the key down if the cover is closed, dumbass?"

The commotion had attracted the attention of the younger costar and his own cameraman, who both hustled over.

"What's going on?" asked the kid.

"The piano played by itself, Ray, I swear to God."

The kid, or Ray, inspected the piano with his flashlight. "The cover is closed."

"Thank you, Einstein," said Ponytail, and took a deep breath and collected himself. He turned to his cameraman. "How did I look?"

"Scared shitless. And that was before you landed on me. The shot is wasted."

"Fine. Let's do another take. We can edit the piano key being struck later, too."

And I proceeded to watch a rather amusing display of TV magic. On the second take, Ponytail once again ran his hand over the closed cover—then feigned hearing the sound. But this time, instead of scrambling for his life, his reaction was much more civilized and under control. He turned his head sharply, opened his mouth in surprise, then cocked his head knowingly, as if he had almost expected the piano to play.

"Good," said the cameraman. "We can use that."

"What's going on?" Jacob asked me. I had nearly forgotten about the boy, and a lot of the fun I was having was lost on him.

"We're having fun," I said.

"We are?"

"Yes," I said. "Watch this."

Ponytail was currently leaning over and watching himself on some replay feature on the camera. I got the sense that he enjoyed watching himself. That he, in fact, lived to watch himself. Liking him less and less, I walked directly into his right shoulder and exited through his left. As I did, his body convulsed nicely.

"What's wrong, Bob?" asked the other cameraman, looking at him.

Ah, so Ponytail had a name.

Bob, aka Ponytail, said, "I don't know, man. Something very cold just went straight through me."

Jacob giggled next to me. "Can I try?"

"Sure," I said.

With a big grin on his face, the boy drifted quickly through Ponytail, entering through his back and exiting through his stomach. Ponytail spasmed instantly.

"Jesus Christ!" said the lead investigator, looking around wildly. "I swear to God it just happened again! Look at my arm! Quick, film it!"

The camera and light swung over to his forearm. I took a peek, too, and never have I seen such glorious goose bumps.

Ray, his young costar, looked at his forearm, too, but with skepticism. "Are you messing with us, Bob?" he asked.

"No, goddammit. I swear to God something went through me twice."

And Jacob went through him yet again.

Ponytail shrieked, spun wildly around, and looked like a cornered hellcat. Except, nothing was cornering him. "It happened again! It's attacking me! Help me, please!"

Jacob giggled some more. I nearly rubbed his damaged head, but stopped myself.

"Nothing's attacking you," said Ray calmly. He turned to one of the cameramen. "Is the air-conditioning on or something?"

The cameraman swiped his hand in front of a vent in the floor near the altar. "No, it's not on."

Ray looked over at Ponytail. "Should we continue rolling, Bob?"

Ponytail took a few deep breaths, calmed himself, stood a little straighter. "Of course we should continue rolling, dumbass. What the fuck do you think we're here for?"

"Bob," said one of the cameramen, "probably not a good idea to be cussing, you know, in a church."

Ponytail looked like he was about to lay into the guy but decided against it. Instead, he turned to Ray. "Get the EMF detector."

The kid reached inside a pocket and produced a handheld electronic gadget-thingy. Ponytail grabbed it without a thank-you and switched it on. A glowing LCD screen illuminated his face in a soft green glow.

"Point zero one," he said, then lowered the gizmo to the carpeted floor. "Still point zero one. Looks like our base reading is point zero—"

I waved my hand in front of the detector.

"Holy shit! Thirty-four point two! Thirty-nine! It's climbing."

Those numbers got everyone's attention. Ponytail swept the gizmo-thingy around some more—and plunged it straight into my chest.

"Sweet Jesus. Fifty-eight point three!"

He raised the thing as high as my head, then lowered it down to my feet, all the while calling out numbers that seemed to steadily rise. He then moved it away from me, and the numbers lowered.

"Okay," he said, short of breath. He had worked himself up. He then shoved the detector back into my chest, which I found rather rude. "Whatever it is seems to be isolated right here."

"About the height of a man," said Ray.

I stepped to the left.

Ponytail frowned. "Damn, lost it." He swept the detector around some more until he found me a few feet away. "Okay, found it."

Always nice, I thought, *to be referred to as an "it."*

Ray came over and tentatively reached out his hand. His groping fingers found my face. "It's, like, ten degrees colder here," he reported. "A moving cold spot."

Ponytail grinned. "Looks like we found ourselves a live one, boys." He then turned and looked directly into one of the camera lenses. "Here be ghosts."

Oh, brother.

37

Ponytail turned to his young costar. "Walk with me."

The two stepped away from the cameramen. I stepped away with them. Jacob had lost all interest in having fun and was now skipping down one of the aisles, humming to himself. The kid had the attention span of a puppy.

"Look," said Ponytail, whispering to his costar, "I'm no more a ghost detective than I am the president of the United States. I have no fucking clue what I'm doing out here half the time. This is, what, our sixth show? The other shows turned up nothing. The ratings are down, and we need this show in a bad way."

"So you weren't faking any of that?" asked Ray.

"On my mother's grave."

"Your mother is alive."

"Well, then on my grandmother's grave. Look, I swear to you, I felt like something walked through me. Three fucking times. And the piano...I didn't touch a damned thing, I swear to you. The thing played itself."

"Okay, I believe you."

"So what do we do now?" asked Ponytail earnestly, and for a moment, he actually seemed a decent enough guy. "I mean, what do they do on the other shows?"

"They usually talk to it and hope they catch something on their voice recorders, which they call electronic voice phenomena, or EVP."

"Okay, good. Let's do that." And Ponytail immediately reverted back to his old, nauseating self. "But let me do the talking, okay? Obviously, this thing is attracted to me, for some reason." He flipped his hair over a shoulder, heroically accepting the fact that he was the chosen one.

"Sure, whatever," said Ray. "But maybe we should call the others—"

"No others," Ponytail hissed. "This is our show, Ray. We both know who the stars are. Who's gotten the most fan mail so far?"

"I've gotten three or four e-mails from a couple of housewives..."

"Well, that's three or four e-mails more than the other two have gotten," said Ponytail. "Which means zilch." He flipped his long hair back over to his other shoulder for no apparent reason. Maybe his shoulder was cold? Anyway, I was tempted to flip it *back*, but I resisted the urge. Didn't want the guy to shit his pants. At least, not yet. Ponytail went on. "Ray, you seem fairly, you know, sensitive at times. Have you seen or felt anything tonight?"

The kid thought about it, and as he did so, his eyes wandered up to the ceiling, where the red-eyed sentries were watching everything quietly from above. Then his eyes fell directly on me.

"There's definitely something in this room," he said. "But I'm not sure what. Maybe more than one thing."

"If one of them is the dead music teacher," said Ponytail, "maybe we could have her, you know, play the piano or something."

"Whatever is here isn't the dead music teacher."

"How the fuck do you know that?"

"Call it a hunch, but I'm pretty sure they're men, and one of them is standing by us now, listening to us."

"Jesus, you're creeping me out."

The kid shrugged. "Like I said, call it a hunch."

"But there's no reports of a man dying here. Just a kid and the music teacher."

"And the tortured monks," said Ray.

"That was hundreds of fucking years ago," said Ponytail. "C'mon, ghosts don't stick around that long, do they?"

The kid shrugged. "I'm not an expert. I just work here, remember?"

"Okay, fine. Let's go before they start thinking we're up to something," said Ponytail, and he indicated the two cameramen.

As they headed back, with me trailing behind, I spotted Jacob chasing random beams of light from the crew's various cameras and flashlights. I could hear him giggling. At least he was having his own kind of fun.

Lord, I killed the kid and reduced him to the mentality of a feline.

"Roll cameras," said Ponytail when they were back with the others. "Let's see what the hell we've got on our hands."

With cameras indeed rolling, Ponytail cleared his throat and, holding what appeared to be a voice recorder, intoned dramatically, "Is there anyone here with us now?"

I assumed he was talking to me. After a few minutes, Ponytail and the kid looked at each other. The cameramen looked at each other, too, shrugging.

"We're friends," added Ray hopefully. "Just here to chat. Can you tell us your name? Can you tell us who you are and why you're here?"

It's a long story, kid.

"We mean you no harm," said Ponytail. "We're here to, you know, help."

Good to know, I thought, and wondered how Ponytail intended to, you know, help me. The cameramen looked at each other again, shaking their heads. Ponytail looked confused and frustrated. His ponytail was currently resting over his right shoulder like a sleeping pet snake.

"Can you give us a sign?" he asked again.

And so I did.

38

I once again drew energy from the camera, and once again, it flickered. When I was sufficiently galvanized, I dipped my finger down through the closed piano lid and pressed an ivory key. It might have been the same ivory key, too. Then again, I'm also tone-deaf.

All four jumped at once.

"Aha! See, I told you," said Ponytail, vindicated, excited. He strutted back and forth in front of the piano like an orange peacock, hands on hips. I think he wanted to high-five someone, but no one volunteered.

Ray said, "Maybe there's just something wrong with the piano, you know, like a malfunction or something?"

So I pressed another. Then another.

"Jesus," said one of the cameramen. I noticed his camera was shaking.

And as I kept pressing the keys, the two ghost detectives actually retreated. Some detectives. Ponytail's cameraman was the bravest of the bunch; he walked right up to the piano and, still shooting, flipped open the keyboard cover. I quit playing.

"It stopped," he reported.

Ponytail had gone bone white. Or, more fittingly, ghost white. "Oh...my...God," he said. "That did *not* just happen."

"If I were a betting man," said his cameraman, still standing over the piano, "I would bet that there's a mouse loose among the piano strings."

"There's no way," said Ponytail, recovering quickly. He wasn't going to let anyone steal his ghost story—and thus his ratings. And, perhaps more important, his fan mail. "There's something going on here, something *powerful*."

Ooh, I liked that! *Powerful*. I haven't been called *powerful* in quite some time, if ever.

"I agree," said Ray. "There is something going on here."

"Oh, hell yeah!" said Ponytail, pumping his fist. "Everyone will be talking about this episode. Everyone." He paused. "Make sure you edit that out," he said to no one in particular.

"I still say it's a mouse," said the cameraman.

But Ponytail wasn't listening. He had a sort of faraway look in his eyes that suggested he was already seeing the weekly Nielsen ratings. Perhaps he was already signing his next big contract. Maybe someday he would. But first, he had to get through this night.

"Hey," said Ponytail's cameraman. "I think something just tried to walk through me."

We all turned to look at him. I raised my ghostly eyebrows, curious, since Jacob was at the far side of the room and the three red-eyed sentries were still high above, watching us vigilantly.

"Really?" asked Ponytail, excited.

"Yeah," said the man. "And since I'm such a fat fuck, it's still only about halfway through." He bowled over with laughter. So did the other cameraman. Both nearly dropped their cameras.

"Maybe he's lost," said the other cameraman, gasping, barely getting the words out. "You know, stuck in your fat ass."

Both were nearly crying with laughter. And with the cameras nearly useless, I took the opportunity to draw power from the machines. As I did so, their lights flickered. So much so that everyone turned and looked at them. The laughter immediately stopped.

"Whenever they flicker," said Ray portentously, "something happens."

I materialized before them.

39

For the first time in a long time, all eyes were on me.

I had no idea how much of me had materialized. I had no idea how solid I was, or even if any details had come through. Did I appear as nothing more than a bright light? Or could they see a man standing before them, a man in his midthirties, hair slightly disheveled, bullet wounds dotting his chest and head and neck?

I didn't know, but they sure as hell were seeing *something*.

Ponytail lost it, shrieking as if someone had doused him with gasoline and set him on fire. He turned, started to run, forgot he was on a raised stage, and pitched forward. I heard a dull *crack*.

The image of Jacob falling to his death came to mind instantly. *Jesus, what have I done?*

Miraculously, Ponytail found his feet. Woozy and punch-drunk and bleeding from a sizable head wound, he managed to stumble out of the nave and out through the side door.

The others barely gave him a glance; instead, they just stared at me in openmouthed wonder. One of the cameramen tried his camera, but it wouldn't work. No surprise there, since I was using all its juice.

"Are you guys seeing this?" asked Ray quietly, awe in his voice. Surprisingly, there was little fear.

The cameramen nodded, but Ray didn't notice them; instead, he moved bravely forward and reached out a hand. He gently touched my shoulder.

"So cold," he whispered.

I noticed something glowing in his eyes, something dead center in his pupils. I realized that something was me. It was my reflection. *My reflection.*

I'm real, I thought.

"You were shot in the head," he said, speaking in low tones, as if afraid he might scare me away. "And the neck and chest. All over. Someone killed you."

I nodded, wondering if he could see me nod.

"Who shot you?" he asked.

I shook my head. He didn't need to know that. It wasn't his business, and there was still much I needed to work out with the boy, let alone the brother who killed me.

"Okay, so you don't want to talk about it. I get it. Can I touch you again? I don't want to be rude; I'm not sure what the etiquette is here."

I smiled and nodded. He smiled, too, and gently ran his open hand along my upper arm. When he pulled his hand away, he shivered and said, "Wow, what a rush."

I heard voices from outside the sanctuary. People were coming.

"You gave my friend quite a fright," said Ray.

I nodded gravely. I felt bad.

"He can be a bit of a jerk sometimes, I know," Ray said. "But he's a good guy. He helped get me this job, you know."

We looked at each other some more. The power from the two cameras was nearly depleted, which meant I was running out of energy. Already, I felt myself fading.

"Hey, you're disappearing," he said. "Was it something I said?"

I shook my head. The voices were now just outside the double doors that connected the cathedral to the school. Ray looked over his shoulder at the sounds.

"They're coming," he said, and when he looked back, I was already gone. But not really. I was still standing there before him. Behind him, the two cameramen gaped at the whole scene in wide-eyed wonderment.

And just as the doors burst open, Ray leaned forward and whispered directly into my ear, "You do not belong here, James. It's time for you to go home."

He stepped back and smiled, and I stood there utterly stunned as people and cameras flooded into the nave, led by a very pale Ponytail.

40

It was after dawn by the time the film crew finally packed up and left.

The principal was the last to leave. She looked tired and beaten down, and I didn't blame her. It had been a hell of a night, and I certainly hadn't helped things by scaring Ponytail half to death. I still felt bad for him. He didn't deserve that.

I was alone. Jacob was off playing in one of the classrooms. It was the weekend, so he would be playing alone. Early-morning light filtered down through the many stained-glass windows, casting a kaleidoscope of colors across the pews. I liked the display of colors and could watch them all morning long, which I often did.

High up on the far wall, above the sanctuary and above the crucifix of Christ and the massive painting of the Mount of Olives, an amorphous shadow separated from the deeper, darker shadows of the ceiling. The shadow took shape, formed arms and legs, and crept slowly down the wall. It stopped between the painting and the crucifix.

And waited.

It was their way of inviting me to join them. Often, I answered their call, rising up to be with them, disappearing into them, my individual thoughts ceasing to exist as I merged into The One.

And their thoughts, more often than not, were centered on protecting that damn painting.

"And they've done a marvelous job of it, haven't they?" said a humor-filled voice just below the entities.

Not too many things surprised me these days—this did.

The only thing below the entities was, of course, the statue of Jesus Christ hanging on the cross. At the moment, it appeared to be trying to pull free one of its nailed hands.

Sweet Jesus.

"Exactly," said the statue. "Now, how about giving a brother a hand?"

41

The statue didn't wait for my help.

As I stared up in stunned silence, incapable of moving even if I had wanted to help, the statue went to work freeing its nailed hands from the cross. As it did so, the three red-eyed beings scuttled quickly away and huddled together in the far corner of the room. I nearly scuttled away with them.

At least I'm not the only one seeing things, I thought.

The statue made a fist with its right hand, gripping the nail head in reverse, so to speak, and began working the spike back and forth, crying out as he did so. When the nail finally came free, the statue bellowed like a wounded and dying animal.

Sweet Jesus.

He did the same with his other hand, grunting and gasping, and when it came free, he found himself balancing precariously on the single nail driven through both his feet. Balancing in that position as rivulets of sweat poured down his damaged body, he plucked each nail from the center of his palms like a magician performing a macabre magic trick. He dropped the bloodied spikes to the carpeted dais below, where they clamored and bounced and came to rest side by side.

Had I been human, I would have vomited violently.

Next, he reached up and gripped the crown of thorns encircling his head. "Man alive, this thing gives me the worst headache." He carefully pushed up, and as fresh blood poured from newly opened wounds, the crown came free. He tossed it aside, and it landed next to the two stakes.

The statue, sucking wind, looked down at me. "This is where I could really use your help, James."

His words ripped through me, snapping me to attention, and in a daze, I found myself warily floating up to him.

"I don't bite, James," he said, and gave me a lopsided smile. His lips, I saw, were badly split, and some of his bottom teeth were broken near the gums. He motioned to the nail driven through his feet. "I could probably pull it out myself, but, well, my back is seriously killing me."

I nodded dumbly and reached for the nail head and wondered how much I could truly help, since I was a ghost.

"Just do your best, James," he said.

I nodded dumbly again and took hold of the nail—and noticed I had solidified enough to wrap both hands around its head. Bracing my bare feet on either side of the cross, I pulled with all my strength, and as I pulled, it slowly came free. Warm blood poured over my knuckles.

Warm blood. On my knuckles.

As I continued to pull, Jesus Christ braced his arms against the thick wooden crossbeam, holding himself up, grunting through clenched teeth. His legs, I saw, were crisscrossed with raw, open wounds. Lash marks.

I pulled with all my strength, grunting myself. And when the nail finally came free, blood sprayed in a crimson arch, glinting in the multicolored morning light shining in through the stained-glass windows.

My God.

The iron spike, slick with blood, slipped from my fingers and bounced and rolled and came to rest next to the others.

"Thank you," said the man, or statue, in front of me. I looked up into his face; he winked at me. "You're a real lifesaver." He then gave me another lopsided grin and dropped down from the cross. He landed loudly on the raised stage.

I drifted down from the cross while he spent a few moments bending and stretching his back. As he did so, something caught his eye in the far corner of the room.

"Wait here, James. I'll be back in a moment."

42

For someone who had been hanging around for unknown decades, he moved surprisingly well—and even looked pretty good in a loincloth.

Crisscrossing his back were dozens of open wounds.

Cat-o'-nine-tails.

Some of the torn flesh was literally flapping free with each step. But if he was in any pain, he didn't show it.

He walked swiftly over to the far corner of the chapel, until he stood directly beneath the three red-eyed sentries. The beings, which were shifting agitatedly high above, watched him restlessly, churning, moving in and over each other, their red eyes flashing warily. Where one began and another ended was nearly impossible to tell. Christ—or, more accurately, the *living statue of Christ*—spoke to them. What he said, I didn't know, but it seemed to calm them down.

They slowed their fidgeting, then stopped altogether.

He said something else to them, and they looked at each other, and I knew they were silently conferring together. They came to some sort of decision, because a moment later, a single shadowed being emerged from The One and crawled tentatively down from the wall.

I watched, stunned. Never had I seen the brothers separate.

And when he was just above Christ's head, he stopped and reached out a shadowed hand from the wall...

Christ reached up and took it, and when the two hands were together, something miraculous happened. That is, something *else* miraculous happened on a night of a thousand miracles.

The shadowed hand turned into a very real hand. And the shadowed being turned into the brilliantly glowing spirit of a real man. A bald man wearing a long, flowing robe. A robe that was riddled with bullet holes.

My God.

Still holding Christ's hand, the monk drifted down from the wall and immediately buried his face in Christ's shoulder, sobbing uncontrollably as Christ hugged him tightly.

In that moment, the golden tunnel appeared in the ceiling above. It glowed invitingly, serenely, and I watched as dozens of spirits emerged from it, surrounding Christ and the monk. One of the spirits, a young man—the fourth brother, perhaps—covered in what appeared to be splashes of paint, embraced the monk in a massive bear hug. When they separated, another spirit, a middle-aged woman, took the monk gently by the hand and led him up to the tunnel in the ceiling.

The monk never looked back, and a moment later, he was gone.

Christ repeated the process with the next brother; a moment later, a slightly taller monk was standing before Christ. After a deep hug of his own, this second monk was led away as well.

After the third and final monk had been led off, the portal in the ceiling disappeared, along with the dozens of spirits.

"That went rather well," said Jesus Christ, looking up, hands on his hips. He then turned to me and said, "We need to talk, James."

43

We sat together in the front pew.

It was still early morning, and the three red-eyed spirits were gone. The place felt oddly empty without them creeping above. Jacob was still off playing somewhere, probably in one of the empty classrooms.

"Indeed," said Christ. "In fact, he's sitting in his old classroom now, pretending to be a student, although sometimes he really thinks he is a student, and wonders where the other kids are."

"How do you know this?" I asked.

Christ smiled patiently at me. "It's easy to do, James, once you know how."

"What's easy to do?"

"Being dead," he said. "Although, I would argue that you are very much *not* dead. Anyway, it has its advantages."

"Death has its advantages?" I asked.

"Sure."

"Such as?"

"Well, knowing where others are at all times, for one. Being connected to anyone and everyone you wish to be connected to."

"I wish to be connected to my daughter," I said. "But I'm not."

"You are. You just don't know it yet."

"I don't understand."

"You have chosen to experience death in this…limited manner," Christ said.

"What limited manner?"

"As what you call a 'ghost.'"

I thought about that. "So I can choose another way?"

"You can choose any way you want."

Morning sunlight crept over the pews. Some of the light found his right leg and revealed clearly his many deep wounds. I looked away. I still hadn't asked him who the hell he really was, although I seriously doubted he was Christ.

I mean, come on, he was just a statue, wasn't he?

I looked up at the cross on the wall. At the *empty* cross.

Yeah, I'm going insane.

"No, you're not," said Christ, reading my thoughts. "And don't be so hard on yourself."

"But I just watched a statue come to life," I said. "I just watched *you* come to life. I think I'm entitled to some crazy talk."

"Hey, and I'm sitting next to a ghost. Maybe we're both a little nuts."

Despite myself, I laughed. He did, too. His laughter was rich and booming, and as he laughed, more blood poured free from his many open wounds.

"You're bleeding all over the pew," I said.

He looked down. "So I am."

I looked at the lash marks covering his legs and torso. "Are you in pain?"

"I'm in whatever I choose to be in," he said. "And if I choose to be in pain, then, yes, I imagine I would be in considerable pain."

I needed some real answers or I was seriously going to lose it. "Were you or were you not just a statue?"

"I chose to be something that would get your attention," he said. "And I think I have succeeded."

"Are you really Jesus Christ?"

"For the sake of simplicity, I will just say yes."

"And what's the complicated answer?" I asked.

"I have been called many things by many people in many languages, throughout time and space, for eons upon eons—"

"Okay, let's stick with the simple answer."

He smiled, nodded. As he did so, beads of blood worked free from his damaged scalp and dribbled down into his ear.

"Is there any way we can get you to stop bleeding?" I asked. "I find it very distracting."

He smiled and nodded again, and by the time he was done nodding, his body had completely healed. Even the blood that had stained the carpet around his feet was gone.

"So you really are Jesus Christ?" I asked. "Please. Just the simple answer."

"The simple answer—of course, James."

"The same Jesus Christ I worshipped as a child?"

"The one and only."

"Are you really the son of God?" I asked.

"We are all children of God," he said. "Although some of us are, let's just say, *older* children of God."

I think I understood. "And you are an older child. Perhaps the oldest of them all."

He smiled easily. "Old or young, James, we are all sons and daughters of the Creator."

The church was quiet, a rarity for this time of day. Perhaps there was some divine intervention going on here. Christ sat motionless next to me, although his chest rose and fell steadily. He was solid, real. Me, not so solid.

"Am I going to hell?" I asked suddenly.

He turned his head slowly, and I could feel the palpable weight of his stare on me. I could feel his love, too. But I also felt something else coming from him.

Sadness.

"I'm sorry, James," he said gently. "But, yes, you are going straight to hell."

44

A door opened somewhere. Probably the morning maintenance crew going about their job. Or Jacob doing a hell of a good job of haunting up the place.

"So that's it, then," I said.

"I'm afraid so, yes."

"Is it as bad as they say?"

"Worse."

"Fuck," I said. "Sorry."

"Cuss all you want, my friend. You've reached the point where it really doesn't matter anymore."

"So I'm beyond help?"

"Yes. Again, I'm sorry."

"So basically I could sin all I want—"

"Right. And it wouldn't matter."

"Fuck."

"Yes, that's the spirit."

"Fuck, fuck, fuck!"

A moment later, after my little tirade, we sat together in silence. Had I been in the flesh, my chest would have been heaving.

Christ said, "Bob didn't deserve what you did to him."

"Bob?" I asked distractedly; after all, my thoughts were on flames and torture and eternal damnation.

"Ponytail," he said.

"Oh, him," I said dismissively.

But Christ pushed on. "He's a real piece of work, I know, but he's coming along. Making some great progress, truly evolving."

"Look, Jesus. I mean no disrespect, but I could give a damn—"

But Christ plunged forward, cutting me off. "He has a girl dying of cancer. Bob really needs this job, and he really needs this show to be a hit. If this show takes off, he can give his little girl the care she's going to need."

"And that's an excuse for him acting like an asshole?" I asked.

"Yes and no," said Christ.

But my mind was still on burning beds, burning caves, burning devils laughing at my misery. I thought of pain. Eternal pain.

"If I'm going to hell," I said, changing the subject, "then I'd rather stay here, in this church, and lose my mind."

"That's your choice, too," said Christ.

"Good. Then that's what I choose."

"So be it," said Christ.

"Just like that?" I said.

"Yes, just like that."

We were silent some more, but I found his words tumbling through my nonskull. "Wait. You said I could choose to experience death any way I want."

"I did indeed."

"But you also just said I was going straight to hell."

"And you were, until you just decided otherwise. I believe your choice was to haunt this church and lose your mind. Admittedly, it wouldn't be my first choice, but to each his own."

"Then why did you say I was going to hell?" I asked.

"Because you *were* going to hell, James. You had already condemned yourself there."

"I don't understand."

"In death, the soul experiences what the soul *wants* to experience."

"But I didn't want to go to hell."

"True enough. But you condemned yourself there anyway."

"But I was told there was a heaven and a hell."

"You were told wrong."

I sat back, stunned. "But I was told by *you*, in the Bible, and by my priests, everyone."

"My words were misconstrued."

"I think you're the Devil," I said suddenly.

"You may think what you want, my son, but the path you are on surely leads to hell."

"Fuck."

"You can say that again."

But I didn't. Instead, I was mulling over his words. "And what would happen if I chose not to believe you?" I asked. "What would happen if I really did go to hell?"

"Well, then I would imagine you would be highly uncomfortable."

"And when I was done being uncomfortable?"

"Then you would leave," he said, patting my hand, "and go to your intended home."

"Intended home?" I asked.

"Yes."

"What kind of home?"

"Let's call it a place of healing. A place of respite. You need a lot of healing, my son."

He patted my hand again, and his warmth radiated through me, and I suddenly wanted to hug him, whoever he was.

"Then hug me," he said.

And so I did. I hugged him with all the strength I had, I hugged him with all my heart and soul, I hugged the man I had been raised to love and to worship. I hugged the man who was even now giving my heart hope.

While I hugged him, he whispered into my ear, "My son, heaven awaits."

And that's when I wept.

45

"You have other questions for me," said Christ.

Morning light came through the stained-glass windows and alighted on him. His skin shone milky white, pure, untouched. He had an elbow propped up on the back of the pew.

"I do," I said. "Just a few."

He looked at me steadily, love in his eyes, a touch of humor. "You want to know if I answer prayers. If so, you want to know why I seem to answer some prayers and ignore others. You want to know if I did indeed perform all those miracles in the Bible. If so, you want to know *how* I performed all those miracles in the Bible. You want to know all of this and more. Much, much more."

"No," I said. "I just want to know if the Lakers will win this year."

He burst out laughing, slapping my shoulder. His hand, amazingly, did not pass through my shoulder. It was a real slap. Real touch. Real interaction.

"Not this year," he answered, "but soon."

I savored his touch. Savored his laughter. I felt like a son sitting next to his father, like a younger brother sitting next to his older brother, a friend sitting next to his best friend—all rolled into one.

"Yes," I said, when the laughter had subsided. "Yes, I have all those questions and more."

"Then I ask you to wait for the answers. Your answers will come soon enough. All of them and more."

I sighed and nodded.

He asked, "Would you care to know why you experienced my touch just now?"

"Yes."

"Because you chose to, James. You *wanted* to feel my touch, and so you did."

"Just like that?" I asked.

"Just like that."

He leaned back on both elbows and closed his eyes and seemed to relish the warmth coming from the colorful beams of sunlight. I had a sense he had not taken a human form in quite a while.

I said, "I'm going to have to journey through the tunnel."

He nodded. "That would be your first step, yes."

"But I have business here," I said. "Unfinished business. With the boy and his brother."

Christ regarded me with his dark-brown eyes, and some of the humor left, replaced by deep love and even deeper concern. "Ah, yes, Jacob," he said. "May I ask a favor of you, James?"

"Of course."

"Will you help me bring him home? He trusts you, you know."

"But I killed him."

"You are going to have to ask for his forgiveness."

"Will he forgive me?"

"Try him. He's a good kid."

A wave of new guilt threatened to overwhelm me. I fought it back. "I'll do my best to bring him…home."

"It's okay to feel guilty," said Christ. "You did end his life, James. But his life was not ended prematurely. Remember that. The two of you are bound together, to the very end—or at least to the end of this story."

"And where does this story end?"

"Wherever you want it to, James."

"What about his brother? What do I do about him?" I asked. "He did, after all, kill me."

"What do you think you should do?"

I thought about that. "I don't hate him, nor do I wish him ill. I know I caused his current mess. I can't imagine what it must have been like for him to lose his brother at such a young age—especially a twin."

"Eli's guilt threatens to overwhelm him, too," said Christ. "He feels responsible for his brother's death. At the very least, Eli feels he should have been the one to fall to his death rather than his innocent brother."

"'Tis a tangled web," I said.

Christ smiled at me. His teeth, I noticed, were small and white. "Not as tangled as you might think."

"So what do I do about Eli?" I asked.

"You'll know when the time comes."

I had suspected he would say that. I changed the subject, as I sensed my time with him was coming to an end. "What happened to the three guardians?"

"Ah," he said. "Although they did an admirable job watching over their brother's painting, the time had come for them to return home, too."

"But how did you convince them to go?" I asked.

"I told them *I* would watch over their painting. Their work here was done." Jesus suddenly stood and stretched his arms. "Now, will you help me back up on the cross?"

"Back on the cross?" I asked, perplexed.

"Yes, James. It's time for me to go, too."

But I didn't want him to go. I wanted him to stay, and comfort me, and keep telling me everything would be okay.

"I'm always here, James," he said, reading my thoughts, patting my back. "Always. You need only to look up."

He then strode quickly across the raised stage and, once under the empty cross, in a surprising feat of dexterity, pulled himself up onto a brass light sconce and grabbed the crossarm of the cross.

"Be a good man, James," he said, looking over his shoulder, "and get me one of the nails. I laid them out nicely for you."

I stared at him briefly, then rose up from the pew and fetched one of the nails. I drifted over to his side.

"This next part might be a little difficult for you, James, so I need you to be strong for me, okay?"

"Okay."

"I need you to drive the nails back in."

He waited. I looked at him. He smiled at me. His eyes twinkled, but he was serious.

I nodded.

"Yeah," I said. "I can do this."

"Good," he said. "Then let's do it. Now."

46

And so I did.

Christ braced himself. He wrapped his left arm around the crossbeam of the cross and positioned his right hand over the hole in the wood, the same hole the nail had been removed from earlier. He nodded to me. Already, there were small beads of sweat on his brow and upper lip.

I felt sick as I positioned the iron stake in the center of his palm. As I did so, the tip briefly touched his flesh, and his hand spasmed slightly.

I can't do this.

I gathered my wits. He watched me carefully, sucked some air, then nodded.

It was time.

Using the heel of my right palm like a hammer, I drove the spike straight through his hand and into the wood behind him.

He jerked and arched his back and cried out loudly.

I wanted to run. I wanted to vomit. I wanted to be anywhere but here. Blood seeped immediately from the new wound in his palm, around the edges of the thick spike. Sweat now poured down his cheeks. His skin was clammy; he looked deathly.

"The other nail, James," he said, gasping. "Please."

I knew he could choose to experience pain, and I also knew he could choose *not* to experience pain. So why did he choose to feel pain now? I suspected I knew.

I quickly fetched the second nail. As I moved over to his right hand, he shook his head. Amazingly, he smiled through gritted teeth.

"No, James. The feet are next."

I drifted down to his bare feet. He had positioned them already, the left over the right. Both feet were shaking, perhaps with anticipation of what was to come.

"Now, James. Do it now. Please."

Once again using the flat of my hand, I drove the stake as hard and as deep as I could through the top of his left foot. But the nail went only so far, and I was forced to keep pounding and pounding until it punched all the way through his right foot and into the wood behind. All the while, he cried out, and blood poured over my hands and knuckles and down the center beam of the cross.

He gasped, hyperventilating.

"Are you okay?" I asked, looking up, completely shaken.

"Always," he said, sucking air. "Always."

I quickly retrieved the third and final nail. His right hand was already in place, and without hesitation, I drove the spike through his palm and into the cross. He screamed and convulsed, and when he finally found his voice again, he gasped, "The crown, James. Mustn't forget the crown."

"Please, I can't—"

"It's okay, James," he said through clenched teeth. "I promise you. It's okay."

The crown was still caked with dried blood and bits of skin. I held it in both hands and brought it back to Jesus Christ.

He smiled at me weakly. "Don't feel bad, okay? I'm just a statue, remember?"

"I find that hard to believe."

"There are people coming, James."

Indeed, I now heard voices approaching, too. Morning Mass was about to start.

"Will I see you again?" I asked.

He took in some air, and his ribs pushed out against his bare chest. I noticed that the bloody slashes and gashes had returned. The spear wound in his side was back as well, dribbling blood and water.

He looked at me and winked. "I'll see you on the other side."

And with that, I lowered the crown of thorns down onto his scalp. At his insistence, I pressed it all the way down to his forehead, just above his eyes, opening deep and ghastly wounds along the way. Blood poured into his eyes and down his face and into his ears and nose and mouth.

"Thank you, James," he said.

The heavy oak door behind me creaked open, and I turned and saw a priest nervously step into the sanctuary. He flipped on some lights.

And when I turned back to Christ…

He was gone, replaced by an ancient painted wooden statue, complete with cracks and dust and cobwebs.

47

Many days passed after that incident, and still I had not worked up the courage—or nerve—to speak with Jacob.

My memory seemed stronger since my encounter with Christ, and often, I drifted up to the statue to study it more closely. Had it really come to life? Was he really in there somewhere? Or had my mind played a massive and not very kind trick on me?

The wooden statue looked as ancient as ever. Hell, it was even rotting in some sections. Interestingly, the nails themselves were made of wood, too. Definitely not the iron spike I had driven through the soft flesh of his palms.

You single-handedly crucified Christ.

Lord, help me.

Real or not, trick or not, I had come face-to-face with *something* overwhelming and powerful, *something* that had given me peace of mind. And *something* that had given me the promise of heaven.

Also, the three red-eyed sentries were gone, so that fact alone was proof that something had indeed happened.

Maybe it was the Devil, come to collect their souls?

I doubted it. I would always remember Christ's love, his overwhelming and powerful love for me. Could the Devil even love? Could the Devil even *fake* love? I doubted it.

Was the Devil even real?

I didn't know, but what I did know was this: Jesus Christ was here. He spoke to me, reassured me. Died for me.

I would often find Jacob alone at night in the various classrooms, raising his hand to answer unasked questions, pretending to drink from the classroom water fountain, playing games alone, singing alone, coloring and writing alone. He also did this when school was in session, and a couple of very sensitive kids watched him from the corner of their eyes. And, of course, they would watch me, too.

Perhaps a week after my encounter with Christ, Pauline came by one evening to see me. She wasn't alone.

She had brought Jacob's twin brother, Eli.

My killer.

48

Pauline and Eli sat together at the far end of a pew about halfway down the center aisle.

They were the only ones in the chapel, but I knew that could change at any given moment. As they sat, Pauline spied me watching them from the stage. She whispered something in Eli's ear. He nodded imperceptibly, and she left him there in the pew and came over to where I was standing, near the altar.

"I see you brought a guest," I said.

Pauline dropped to her knees and bowed her head as if praying. Maybe she was praying, but certainly not to me. She was, I saw, feigning prayer.

"You seem somehow different, stronger," she said. As she spoke, her lips barely moved. To the average person, she appeared only to be whispering a prayer.

"Well, I had a little talk with someone," I said.

She glanced up at me sharply, scanning my thoughts, then flicked her gaze up to the statue of Jesus Christ hanging above us. Her mouth dropped open. "You have got to be kidding."

"The one and only," I said.

She shook her head, grinning, then looked at me some more. "You look better, James. Brighter, iridescent."

"Iridescent?" I laughed. "Yes, I feel better. And my memory is coming back, too."

I looked over her shoulder at the young man sitting alone with his head bowed and hands clasped before him. He could have been any other worshipper, except I knew for a fact that he had shot me in cold blood and murdered Mrs. Randolph with his own hands. Seeing him again, in the flesh, was fairly emotional for me.

"I take it your private investigator was successful," I said.

"Oh, yes. Found him still living at home. His mother is a wreck. Whole family is a wreck. All of it dates back to the death of Jacob."

Great. Killed a kid and ruined an entire family in the process. How the hell was I *not* going to hell?

"Get a grip on yourself," she said, listening to my thoughts.

I did and focused instead on Christ's last request of me: to help Jacob move on.

I can do this, I thought.

Pauline continued. "Yes, the family is in a helluva mess, a mess they can't seem to climb out of. The father divorced the mother a decade ago, and the surviving twin, our boy Eli, has been selling drugs and stealing cars ever since to support her."

"Shit," I said.

"It gets worse."

"Great."

"Hang in there," she said. "He was caught selling drugs in his early twenties and spent five years in jail. He got out two years ago."

"Two years ago was when I was killed," I said.

"Yes."

"Which would explain why he had waited so long for his revenge."

"I suppose so," she said.

"And what about my partner in crime?" I asked, and amazingly, his name was coming back to me. "Dustin something or other?"

"Yes, Dustin Hicks, the boy who helped you drag Jacob up to the rafters. He was murdered outside his apartment two years ago, too. Unsolved."

"So Eli got us both."

"Appears so," she said. "But that didn't necessarily make things any better for him. In fact, it probably made things even worse. My PI friend says that word on the street is that this kid owes a lot of money to the wrong people and is in some serious shit."

"Which explains why he came looking for a wad of cash he remembered hiding on that fateful day," I said. "The cash in my wallet."

"And hocking the church relics," added Pauline. "By the way, what were you doing with all that money in your wallet, anyway?"

I remembered. I remembered with almost perfect clarity. Wonderful, electrifying clarity.

"I was on the high school football team," I said. "Part of being on the team meant we had to sell advertising for our weekly football program. One of our sponsors had given me cash the day before. I was going to turn it in."

"And you probably showed it off to someone."

I nodded. Seemed about right.

"And Eli probably saw you do it," she said. "You must have left your wallet lying around—"

"It was in my gym locker. He busted into it."

"Fine. He breaks into your locker, steals it. Someone spots him do it but fingers the wrong twin. And you go after the wrong brother, and..."

She stopped for a breath. Thank God. I looked over at Eli, who was still seated with his head bowed, a miserable wreck of a man. A drug addict, a drug dealer, an ex-con, a killer, and now an only son...

"And the rest is history," I finished.

49

"So how did you get him to come here?" I asked Pauline. "And why, exactly, is he here?"

"You know why he's here, James."

"I do?"

"If not, then you will," she said. She was still on her knees and still subvocalizing beneath her breath, her voice audible only to God and me. I felt special. "And as far as how I got him here—easy. I confronted him about the murders."

"Confronted alone?"

"No, the private investigator was with me. Luckily, the guy doubles as a bodyguard. He's waiting in the foyer, by the way. Anyway, I approached Eli about everything. To say he was shocked was an understatement."

"How did you explain catching him?"

"Told him we had a witness in the church."

"How did you explain your involvement?" I asked.

"I didn't. Not really. He was rather shocked and numb and probably a little high on whatever it was he had last taken. He didn't ask who I was or how I was involved."

"So how did you get him to come down here?"

Pauline smiled. She looked tired. I could see this had taken a lot out of her. Confronting a serial killer, I was sure, had been stressful.

"You bet your ass it was stressful," she said. "You owe me big, mister. Maybe you can ask your friend Jesus to toss me a miracle or two."

I grinned. "I'll see what I can do."

She went on. "So I told Eli, quite bluntly, that I was a medium and that his brother was still haunting the church of his death and that he, Eli, needed to do something about it."

"And Eli believed you?"

"He's here now, isn't he?"

"Okay, so he believed you," I said. "What's next?"

"That," she said, "is between you, Eli, and Jacob. And maybe the police. And maybe even God."

50

At Pauline's request, I retrieved Jacob from one of the school hallways, where I found him trying unsuccessfully to drink from a water fountain.

Now the four of us were standing near the altar, the scene of so much pain and suffering. To the naked eye, of course, there would have appeared to be just two people standing there.

Pauline was holding Eli's hand, which should have surprised me but didn't. I felt neutral toward Eli. Yes, I had taken much from him, but that had been a reckless, stupid accident. Eli, on the other hand, had hunted me down and killed me in cold blood. *Tit for tat.*

Jacob was by my side, and his little face was screwed up in utter bewilderment as he took in the scene. On some level, I knew the boy recognized his twin brother, but I also knew that Jacob saw Eli as his music teacher's killer. I sensed the kid's confusion and conflicting emotions. I looked from one to the other. It was hard to imagine that these two had once been identical twins. I had taken so much away from them. One was so young and bloodied, and the other so much older and damaged. One had stopped growing in death, while the other had marched on into misery.

"They're both here," said Pauline gently to Eli.

For the first time since entering the church, Eli raised his head. "Who's here?" he asked. His voice was soft yet hoarse. A smoker's voice. A screamer's voice. The voice of someone who had neglected his body in one way or another.

"Your brother," said Pauline. "And James, one of the men you killed."

A mélange of emotions crossed his face at once: doubt, amusement, fear. In the end, I think he settled on dubious trepidation. He was still a handsome guy. Dark hair, flecked with premature gray, perhaps indicative of a life not very well lived. He was also not very tall. Pauline had him by a few inches, which might have given her a false sense of security. Indeed, Eli had wide, round shoulders. Strong for his size.

He said, "You mean, you know, like, here from the other side? Like in that show *Crossing Over*?" As he spoke, he did so with a pseudo-Brooklyn tough-guy accent. Except, I knew he had lived in LA most of his life.

"Close, Eli. These two never crossed over. They have been with us ever since."

"I don't understand," he said. The Brooklyn tough guy was gone in an instant.

"Your brother has been haunting this church since his death, Eli. For nearly twenty years."

The bigger twin suddenly looked sick. He also looked like he needed to sit down.

Pauline pushed on. "And James never passed on, either."

"Never passed on?" he asked weakly, confused.

"Crossed over," she explained.

"Where...Where are they?"

"Standing by my side."

He looked to her side, at a place somewhere in between Jacob and me.

"Bullshit," he said. "I don't fucking believe it."

He adjusted his shoulders. The tough guy was back. The street drug dealer, the ex-con, the killer. But Pauline was a tough girl, too, and she was unafraid. I also knew she preferred not to waste her time convincing skeptics, but apparently, this case was different.

"Eli, your brother is standing next to the man you killed. They are both looking at you. Your brother is wearing a school uniform. Dark pants and a short-sleeved white dress shirt. The dress shirt is covered in blood from a massive head wound. His neck also appears as if it might be broken. Your brother understands very little of what is happening presently. Young spirits are often confused, and he is very, very confused, Eli. He needs your help to move on."

And as she spoke, the drug-dealing, murderous ex-con slowly broke down. I saw his face change shape. The hard lines softened. The lower lip quivered. Eyes watered.

She pressed on without pause. "And the man who accidentally killed your brother is here, too. The man you, out of revenge, killed in return. James is standing next to Jacob."

Eli got hold of himself at the mention of my name. Pauline was in a near trancelike state now that she was truly locked in to the two spirits in the room. Sometimes I took her mediumship for granted. I knew such focused concentration took a lot of effort.

"James is really here?" said Eli.

"Yes, Eli. He really is."

But he still didn't seem entirely convinced. He also didn't seem entirely stable, either.

"What about Dustin Hicks?" he asked.

"Dustin passed over long ago and is not here, although he is taking an active interest in this from afar."

Oh, really? I thought. Pauline never ceased to amaze me.

"Thank you," she said to me.

"What?" said Eli.

"Nothing," said Pauline.

But Eli wasn't really paying attention. Instead, he was focused on the spot between Jacob and me. Sweat had formed across his brow, and he was absently cracking his neck, rolling his head around on those wide shoulders. I could only imagine that his neck was tense as hell.

"What about the old lady?" he asked.

"Mrs. Randolph?" asked Pauline. "Whom you murdered a few months ago?"

I didn't know a murderer could look sheepish, but Eli managed to do so now, ducking his head a little. "Um, yeah, her."

"She's not here, either. She has passed over and is taking no interest in this."

He opened his mouth to speak, but nothing came out, so he closed it again and hunched his shoulders some more.

"From what I understand," said Pauline, cocking her head and listening to voices even I couldn't hear, "she has forgiven you and holds no ill will toward you for taking her life."

He opened his mouth to speak again, and this time he was successful. "I never meant to kill her, you know."

"She knows."

He cracked his neck again. "So James and my brother are really here now?"

"Yes," said Pauline.

"Is there, um, any chance they can give me a sign or something?"

"Your brother doesn't understand the concept of 'giving a sign,' Eli, but James might oblige."

He nodded. "Fine. Could you, um, ask him for me?"

"He's right here, listening to you," she said. "What would you like him to do?"

"I dunno. Maybe move something."

There was a silver candlestick holder on the altar. I took Eli's hand, drew energy from him, and promptly pushed over the candlestick. It landed with a thunderous *clang*, and Eli jumped back.

"Holy sweet Jesus!" He gripped his chest and looked at his forearm, which was now completely covered in gooseflesh—a result, no doubt, of my grabbing his hand. "Is he going to hurt me?"

"Are you going to hurt him?" Pauline asked me.

"Of course not," I said.

"He says, 'Of course not.'"

Eli had backed up all the way to the edge of the stage. He looked as if he might bolt at any moment.

"Tell him to come back," I said to Pauline.

She repeated my request to him.

Eli did so, grudgingly. He said, "Tell James no more, you know, proof. I believe he's here."

I sighed. Scaring the hell out of him had been, admittedly, kind of fun.

"So what now?" Eli asked. There was a little more pep to his voice. Being scared half to death has that effect on people.

"Now," said Pauline, "is when things get interesting."

51

"First of all," said Pauline to Eli, "we need to get Jacob up to speed here. He's very confused. Mostly, he recognizes you as Mrs. Randolph's killer, but there's a part of him that thinks he might know you from somewhere else."

"Why…Why doesn't he recognize me?" asked Eli, truly hurt.

"It's the nature of lost souls," said Pauline. "With no real feedback from, well, anyone, they lose sight of themselves, forget who they are, and their memories subsequently go as well."

"He doesn't even remember who he is?" asked Eli, and I could hear the anger and pain in his voice. I was also aware that the anger was probably directed toward me.

"Mostly, he doesn't," said Pauline. "Sometimes he has glimpses of who he is and who he was. But every day he forgets more and more, Eli. Every day the condition worsens."

"You mean, someday he won't even remember who he is?"

"Exactly."

"Then we need to help him," said Eli firmly. "Send him to heaven or something."

"It's not going to be that easy, Eli. Your own father planted the seeds of doubt in the afterlife, which is why he is still here."

Eli didn't say anything at first. Sweat continued to bead along his forehead, and he seemed to be growing paler by the minute. I wondered if he was *ever* going to get his color back. Finally, he started nodding.

"Yeah, Dad was an atheist. Hard-core atheist. Mom wasn't. Dad was against us going to Catholic school from the beginning, but Mom won out. Still, whenever we were alone with him, he would tell us we were wasting his money and that there was no God or heaven or hell. We believed him. Hell, he was our dad— we would have believed anything he said."

"What do you believe now?" asked Pauline.

"I believe there's a ghost in here—a ghost who can fucking knock over a candlestick. That's enough for me."

Pauline nodded. They were silent.

After a moment, Eli asked, "So there really is a heaven and a hell?"

"There is whatever you want there to be, Eli. Your brother believed in no heaven or hell, so he is stuck here, in disbelief."

"Then why is James stuck here?"

"Ah," said Pauline, smiling over at me. "He had the opposite problem."

"Opposite?"

"He believed *too* much."

"I don't get it," said Eli.

"He truly believed he was going to hell, Eli, and he was afraid."

"And why was he afraid of going to hell?" asked the bigger twin. He had inched closer to the altar. Not quite as close as before, but he was growing braver.

"Do you really want to know?" asked Pauline.

"Yes."

"He regrets killing your brother, Eli. Regrets it more than you will ever know."

Amazingly, Eli looked right at me. People are more psychic than they know. He looked and said nothing.

"You didn't have to kill him, Eli. He was killing himself, slowly, surely, much the same way you're killing yourself now."

The young man suddenly covered his face and broke down in tears. Pauline never moved, but Jacob did. The little boy was by his brother's side in an instant, trying unsuccessfully to take his hand.

It was heartbreaking and piteous.

And it was all because of me.

52

"My hand is cold," said Eli between sobs. He opened and closed his hand slowly. I could see the occasional shiver coursing through him.

"It's your brother," said Pauline. "He's trying to hold your hand. He's trying to comfort you."

Eli looked down at his empty hand. "What…What does Jacob look like?"

"Ah," said Pauline. "He's young. Maybe eight years old. Seems sort of small for his age. Hair disheveled. And…" Pauline stopped. I knew she had been about to mention Jacob's wounds but caught herself. "And he loves you. But he still remembers you as his piano teacher's killer, Eli, so you will need to speak with him."

"What do I say?" Eli was still looking at his hand. His forearm was completely covered in gooseflesh.

"First, let's sit."

And Pauline led the way over to the wide first step leading up to the raised stage. She sat and patted the spot next to her. Eli slouched over and sat there.

"Invite your brother," said Pauline.

"How?"

"Just ask him to come over."

Eli looked at her for a moment, clearly trying to decide whether or not she was crazy—or perhaps trying to decide if this was another drug-induced hallucination. Finally, he nodded, resigning himself to accept as true the strange events unfolding around him.

"Jacob..." he said quietly, looking over at Pauline as if to ask, *Is this how I do it?*

She nodded approvingly.

Encouraged, Eli raised his voice. "Jacob, it's me, Eli. Your brother. Come sit with me, okay?"

Jacob didn't move. Instead, he looked at me, eyes wide, mouth open, confused as hell.

"Go on," I urged him. "It's okay."

The confusion turned briefly to fear, then to hope. I encouraged him again, and finally, he drifted over and sat cautiously next to his brother on the carpeted step. All three of them—Pauline, Eli, and Jacob—were now facing out toward the empty church. I stood behind them.

"He's sitting next to you now," said Pauline to Eli.

And, surprising the hell out of me, Eli said, "I know. I...I can feel him."

I moved off the stage and sat before them in the front pew. Pauline glanced over at me. "I owe you big," I said to her.

"I know," she mouthed quietly.

Needing no further prompting from Pauline, Eli said, "Hi, Jacob. I'm your brother, Eli. Do you remember me? We were twins. We *are* twins. We did everything together. Do you remember any of that?"

Jacob, who was about half the size of Eli, looked up at his twin brother in complete confusion.

"Keep going," urged Pauline. "Keep reminding him of who he is. Talk about anything that comes to mind."

And so Eli did. He opened up about everything, especially about their immediate family, speaking at length about their mother and father, repeating names often, telling funny and sad stories. As he spoke, Eli broke down often, fought through the tears, picked up where he had left off, and went on. All the while, he held out his hand for little Jacob to hold on to, which the boy did.

"And I had no idea you were still here, Jacob. If I had known, I would have visited you every day. I'm sorry you were alone for so long. I'm so sorry you lost your memory. I'm so sorry I stole the money and you got blamed. I'm so sorry you got killed. It should have been me. Not you. I'm so, so sorry, so sorry..."

Pauline was in tears. Eli was in tears. And Jacob was hugging his twin brother with all his ghostly strength. After a while, the boy turned and looked back at me.

"This is my brother, Eli," he said excitedly.

I smiled and nodded, and he went back to hugging his brother.

53

"He's hugging you," said Pauline, wiping her eyes.

Eli nodded. He knew. He was getting used to this stuff. He and his brother hugged some more while Pauline and I watched them, saying nothing. Finally, the boy pulled away and looked up at his brother.

"Where have you been, Eli?" asked Jacob.

"He's asking where you've been," relayed Pauline.

Eli, aware that the physical connection with his brother had been broken, sat up a little straighter and dried his eyes on his sleeve. "Tell him—"

"No," said Pauline. "You tell him. He can hear you."

Eli nodded. "I've been away, Jacob."

"Where?"

"He's asking where," said Pauline.

"I've been in jail. I've done some bad things, Jacob. Very bad."

"Why?" asked Jacob.

Pauline repeated the question. Eli, who was still seated, suddenly stood. He ran his hand through his oily, unkempt hair and paced the wide carpeted area between the front pews and the stage.

Eli answered, "It was the only thing I could think to do, Jacob."

We were silent. Jacob was still sitting next to Pauline. He looked up at her. She smiled down at him. He then looked at me, and I smiled, too.

"I don't understand," said Jacob. I wasn't sure whom he was addressing, but I sensed it was my time to step in, and so I did.

I drifted over and settled next to him.

Pauline spoke. "Your brother is still very confused, Eli. James just sat with him."

"Why is James sitting with him?" Eli paused, spitting the question.

"James is here for a reason, Eli. He has his own issues, and he needs to resolve them with Jacob. You need to let this happen. It's okay."

Eli didn't like it, but he resumed pacing. Jacob alternated between watching his brother and watching me.

"I don't understand," Jacob said to me. "Eli keeps telling me I'm dead, but I'm not dead."

Some days were better than others for Jacob. Today was a bad day—he remembered little, if anything, of his death. And it would only get worse for him. If ever there were a correct time for him to move on, now would be it.

Pauline caught my eye and nodded. I knew what she was thinking: *Yes, now is the correct time.*

I said to the boy, "About twenty years ago, Jacob, you fell from up there." I pointed to the rafters above.

Jacob followed my finger. His mouth fell open a little, although he said nothing.

I went on. "Do you remember falling and hitting your head?"

His eyes traced the path from my finger to the altar below. "I...I fell on that?" he asked. It was partly a question, partly a statement.

"Yes, Jacob."

"There was a lot of blood," he said. He was remembering.

"Yes."

"I got killed."

I nodded, unable to speak.

"I was a bad boy," he said.

"No, Jacob," I said. "You were a good boy. I was a bad boy." And so, after many days and weeks and years of living with the guilt—and dying with the guilt—I knew it was time. "Jacob, do you remember the boys who dragged you up to the rafter, the boys who hung you over the edge?"

He scrunched up his little face as he thought back. "There were two of them," he said, and now that he was being prodded, his memory was coming back to him in bits and pieces. Pauline watched us silently, listening, tears in her eyes.

"Yes, two of them," I said. This was going to be harder than I had thought it would be, but I forced myself onward. "Jacob, I was one of those boys."

He looked sharply at me. "I don't understand."

"Jacob, I was one of the two boys who pulled you up to the rafters. I was the one who hung you over it. I was the one who accidentally dropped you."

"But I don't under—"

"Jacob, *I* killed you. It was *me*. I dropped you. I caused you to fall and hit your head. It was me who killed you."

The nave was empty. Outside, in the adjoining halls and rooms, I could hear a vacuum running and the murmur of voices. The main church itself was empty, except for the four of us—two humans and two ghosts.

Jacob said nothing at first. He stared up at me with his head tilted slightly, his little knees pressed together. I couldn't help but notice the ethereal blood from his wound was everywhere: over his collar, down his shirt, even up along his sleeves.

"I'm sorry, Jacob," I said. "I'm so very, very sorry. I didn't mean to kill you. I didn't mean to drop you. I was just trying to scare you, I was just trying to find my wallet, but you had no idea what I was talking about, and you were scared, you were so very scared, but I didn't believe you..."

I broke down completely, weeping into my hands, unable to speak, unable to think, unable to focus, unable to live, unable to die, unable to do anything.

I felt another presence next to me.

It was Jacob, and he had wrapped his arms tightly around me.

54

I was standing with Pauline off to the side of the sanctuary, near the piano, while Jacob and Eli sat together on the stage's top step. Pauline was holding my hand.

"Jacob forgives you, James."

"Yes," I said.

"Now it's time for you to forgive yourself."

"I know."

Jacob was jabbering away nonstop to his brother. Eli gave no indication of hearing him, but if this bothered Jacob, he didn't show it. As I listened in now, Jacob was busy telling Eli about what had happened to him in school on some unknown day in some unknown year. Whether or not the boy had been dead or alive on this school day, I didn't know, and I didn't think Jacob knew, either.

Amazingly, no one had yet stepped inside the church, and I wondered if Pauline's big private eye guarding the outside foyer had anything to do with that.

"Either that or divine intervention," said Pauline, reading my thoughts.

"You think?" I asked.

She grinned. "Nah. Just dumb luck."

I thought of my daughter growing up without me. I thought of my wife moving on without me. I thought of the world spinning around without me. I really *was* dead. I really *was* moving on.

"You can always come back, you know," said Pauline.

"From the dead? I thought that only happened in horror movies."

"Hey, sitting in a creepy old church with a serial killer and two ghosts *is* a horror movie," she said. "For some people."

"But not you," I said. "You're a brave girl."

"Or a stupid girl," she said.

I looked at her. "I couldn't have done this without you, Pauline. Thank you."

"What's a medium to do?"

Pauline and I were quiet some more. Jacob kept talking; he hadn't stopped or slowed down. Eli, for his part, sat still and seemed to revel in the presence of his twin brother.

"When you said I could come back, what did you mean?"

"Reincarnation," she said. "That is, if you choose to come back. Or you can come back in other ways, too. In spirit, in dreams, in thoughts. Not to mention every time your daughter thinks of you or speaks your name or asks for your help, you can instantly be by her side."

"How is that even possible?" I asked, amazed and thrilled by the prospect of seeing my daughter again.

"My dear, there are far greater things in heaven than on earth. You'll just have to ask around up there."

As if on cue, a glow appeared from above. The tunnel had returned.

55

And it was closer and brighter than ever.

From it poured a multitude of friendly, smiling spirits, filling the church sanctuary. Some I thought I recognized, but I couldn't remember them.

Pauline's eyes widened. "Looks like they brought the whole welcoming committee this time."

I nodded nervously. I still hadn't completely wrapped my head around the fact that I was leaving, nor had I entirely escaped the old fears and doubts.

Be strong, James. Be strong.

Eli came over and stood with Pauline, completely unaware that a portal to the heavens had opened above him. Jacob stayed behind on the step, staring wide-eyed at the outpouring of spiritual activity around him. I recalled the boy hiding in fear while Mrs. Randolph was shown the way to the tunnel. This time, Jacob did not run or hide.

There is strength in numbers.

I had learned that lesson from the red-eyed sentries. The boy had been alone before; now he was not.

Jacob looked at me, grinning from ear to ear. "Look at all the angels!" he said, clapping.

"Aren't they beautiful?" I said.

"So beautiful!"

I turned to Pauline. Eli was still standing next to her. I could tell he knew something was going on, that a shift had occurred, that there was something in the air. Boy, was there something in the air.

I said to Pauline, "Tell Eli that I'm so very sorry for killing his brother."

As she did so, Eli turned and looked directly into my eyes. "I'm sorry for killing you, James. I'm sorry for shooting you in your sleep. That was cowardly and wrong, and now I'm going to pay for it."

I told him I forgave him. I told him that he needed to forgive himself, too—words I knew were easier said than done.

Pauline relayed all of this to Eli, who nodded solemnly. She then led him over to his brother, who was now playing catch with a beautiful raven-haired woman, using a glowing orb that looked remarkably like a little sun. I knew this woman. I knew her deeply and passionately and knew I had known her since the dawn of time. She was my soul mate, my passion, my love. I just couldn't remember who the hell she was.

Soon, I thought. *Soon.*

She glanced over her shoulder at me and smiled so brightly that my entire countenance flared briefly, especially over my heart. She went back to playing with Jacob, and I looked up into the golden tunnel above.

So bright. So welcoming. So beautiful. So warm.

So very warm.

I hadn't been warm in a long, long time.

And now I noticed for the first time that a crystal stairway led through the tunnel. I hadn't noticed it before; then again, I hadn't been this close to the tunnel before, either. I thought of my daughter. Would I see her again? I was sure I would, somehow. I thought of hell, and I glanced over at the wooden cross. The statue of Christ was as unmoving as ever, but I smiled at it anyway. Jesus Christ had said everything was going to be okay, and I believed him.

Pauline was by my side again, and this time she was holding little Jacob's hand. She passed it over to me. I took it firmly. Jacob looked up at me and smiled excitedly.

"Are we going home?" he asked.

"Yes," I said. "We're going home."

He bounced and smiled and waved at various spirits flitting about the sanctuary. One was an elderly woman, quite possibly his grandmother.

I looked at Pauline. "I'm a little nervous."

"It's going to be okay, James."

I nodded. I knew it was going to be okay. I knew this in my heart, and I trusted my heart. I also knew it was time to move on. It was time for peace. It was time for rest. It was time for healing.

"Would you do me a favor?" I asked Pauline.

"Anything, James."

I gave her my request, and she immediately nodded and dashed off. A moment later, she returned with the red scarf my daughter had given me.

"It was still there," she said, "hidden in the cushions."

"Please give it back to her, and please tell her that her daddy loves her very much," I said.

"I will, James."

"And please tell her good-bye for me."

"I will, James."

"You're an angel, Pauline."

"I know."

I smiled and looked up into the tunnel again. Remarkably, it seemed even closer, hovering now just above my head. I could see through it almost all the way to the other side. All the way to God.

"So what do I do?" I asked Pauline nervously.

"Do you see the stairs?" she asked.

The crystal stairs had descended now all the way to the church's raised, carpeted platform.

"Yes."

"I'm being told that all you need to do is to start climbing, James, and you will be shown the way. But the first step is your choice. No one will do it for you."

I understood. I gripped Jacob's hand tightly. Pauline was crying softly now. The stairway was just a few feet away.

I'm really doing this, I thought.

"I want to go to heaven," said Jacob excitedly, bouncing up and down next to me. "I want to see Grandma!"

I turned to Pauline. "I love you, you know."

Tears were flowing freely down her cheeks. "I love you, too, James. Now, get going."

I turned back to the stairway. *Yes, I'm really doing this.*

Gripping Jacob's hand, I lifted my bare foot and stepped up onto that first crystal step…And for the first time in a long, long time, I felt warm.

Gloriously warm.

The End

1

I was folding laundry in the dark and watching Judge Judy rip this guy a new asshole when the doorbell rang.

I flipped down a pair of Oakley wraparound sunglasses and, still holding a pair of little Anthony's cotton briefs in one hand, opened the front door.

The light, still painfully bright, poured in from outside. I squinted behind my shades and could just make out the image of a UPS deliveryman.

And, oh, what an image it was.

As my eyes adjusted to the light, a hunky guy with tan legs and beefy arms materialized through the screen door before me. He grinned at me easily, showing off a perfect row of white teeth. Spiky yellow hair protruded from under his brown cap. The guy should have been a model—or at least my new best friend.

"Mrs. Moon?" he asked. His eyes seemed particularly searching and hungry, and I wondered if I had stepped onto the set of a porno movie. Interestingly, a sort of warning bell sounded in my head. Warning bells are tricky to discern, and I automatically assumed this one was telling me to stay away from Mr. Beefy, or risk damaging my already rocky marriage.

"You got her," I said easily, ignoring the warning bells.

"I've got a package here for you."

"You don't say."

"I'll need for you to sign the delivery log." He held up an electronic gizmo-thingy that must have been the aforementioned delivery log.

"I'm sure you do," I said, and opened the screen door and stuck a hand out. He looked at my very pale hand, paused, and then placed the electronic thingamajig in it. As I signed it, using a plastic-tipped pen, my signature appeared in the display box as an arthritic mess. The deliveryman watched me intently through the screen door. I don't like to be watched intently. In fact, I prefer to be ignored and forgotten.

"Do you always wear sunglasses indoors?" he asked casually, but I sensed his hidden question: *And what sort of freak are you?*

"Only during the day. I find them redundant at night." I opened the screen door again and exchanged the log doohickey for a small square package. "Thank you," I said. "Have a good day."

He nodded and left, and I watched his cute little buns for a moment longer, then shut the solid oak door completely. Sweet darkness returned to my home. I pulled up the sunglasses and sat down in a particularly worn dining room chair. Someday I was going to get these things reupholstered.

The package was heavily taped, but a few deft strokes of my painted red nail took care of all that. I opened the lid and peered inside. Shining inside was an ancient golden medallion. An intricate Celtic cross was engraved across the face of it, and embedded within the cross, formed by precisely cut rubies, were three red roses.

In the living room, Judge Judy was calmly explaining to the defendant what an idiot he was. Although I agreed, I turned the TV off, deciding that this medallion needed my full concentration.

After all, it was the same medallion worn by my attacker six years earlier.

Also available on Amazon Kindle:

Dark Horse
A Jim Knighthorse Novel

by
J.R. Rain

(Read on for a sample)

1

Charles Brown, the defense attorney, was a small man with a round head. He was wearing a brown-and-orange zigzagged power tie. I secretly wondered if he went by Charlie as a kid and had a dog named Snoopy and a crush on the little redheaded girl.

We were sitting in my office on a warm spring day. Charlie was here to give me a job if I wanted it, and I wanted it. I hadn't worked in two weeks and was beginning to like it, which made me nervous.

"I think the kid's innocent," he was saying.

"Of course you do, Charlie. You're a defense attorney. You would find cause to think Jack the Ripper was simply a misunderstood artist before his time."

He looked at me with what was supposed to be a stern face.

"The name's Charles," he said.

"If you say so."

"I do."

"Glad that's cleared up."

"I heard you could be difficult," he said. "Is this you being difficult? If so, then I'm disappointed."

I smiled. "Maybe you have me confused with my father."

Charlie sat back in my client chair and smiled. His domed head was perfectly buffed and polished, cleanly reflecting the halogen lighting above. His skin appeared wet and viscous, as if his sweat glands were ready to spring into action at a moment's notice.

"Your father has quite a reputation in LA. I gave his office a call before coming here. Of course, he's quite busy and could not take on an extra case."

"So you settled on the next best thing."

"If you want to call it that," he said. "I've heard that you've performed adequately with similar cases, so I've decided to give you a shot, although my expectations are not very high, and I have another PI waiting in the wings."

"How reassuring," I said.

"Yeah, well, he's established. You're not."

"But can he pick up a blind-side blitz?"

Charlie smiled and splayed his stubby fingers flat on my desk and looked around my office, which was adorned with newspaper clippings and photographs of yours truly. Most of the photographs depict me in a Bruins uniform, sporting the number 45. In most, I'm carrying the football, and in others, I'm blowing open the hole for the tailback. Or at least I like to think I'm blowing open the hole. The newspapers are yellowing now, taped or tacked to the wood paneling. Maybe someday I'll take them down. But not yet.

"You beat SC a few years back. I can never forgive you for that. Two touchdowns in the fourth quarter alone."

"Three," I said. "But who's counting?"

He rubbed his chin. "Destroyed your leg, if I recall, in the last game of the season. Broken in seven different places."

"Nine, but who's counting?"

"Must have been hard to deal with. You were on your way to the pros. Would have made a hell of a fullback."

That *had* been hard to deal with, and I didn't feel like talking about it now to Charlie Brown. "Why do you believe in your client's innocence?" I asked.

He looked at me. "I see. You don't want to talk about it. Sorry I brought it up." He crossed his legs. He didn't seem sorry at all. He looked smugly down at his shoes, which had polish on the polish. "Because I believe Derrick's story. I believe he loved his girlfriend and would never kill her."

"People have been killed for love before. Nothing new."

On my computer screen before me, I had brought up an article from the *Orange County Register*. The article showed a black teen being led away into a police car. He was looking down, his head partially covered by his jacket. He was being led away from a local high school. A very upscale high school, if I recalled. The story was dated three weeks ago, and I remembered reading it back then.

I tapped the computer monitor. "The police say there's some indication that his girlfriend was seeing someone else and that jealousy might have been a factor."

"Yes," said the attorney. "And we think this someone else framed our client."

"I take it you want me to find this man."

"Or person."

"Ah, equality," I said.

"We want you to find evidence of our client's innocence, whether or not you find the true murderer."

"Anything else I should know?"

"We feel race might be a factor here. He was the only black student in school and in the neighborhood."

"I believe the preferred term is African-American."

"I'm aware of public sentiment in this regard. I don't need you to lecture me."

"Just trying to live up to my difficult name."

"Yeah, well, cool it," he said. "Now, no one's talking at the school. My client says he was working out late in the school gym, yet no one saw him, not even the janitors."

"Then maybe he wasn't there."

"He was there," said Charlie simply, as if his word were enough. "So do you want the job?"

"Sure."

We discussed a retainer fee, and then he wrote me a check. When he left, waddling out of the office, I could almost hear Schroeder playing on his little piano in the background.

1

We were at a Starbucks in Silver Lake, which is a hilly district east of Hollywood. Yes, there was even a lake here. Granted, it was a reservoir surrounded by an eight-foot-high chain-link fence topped with barbed wire, but, hey, that's LA for you.

I was eating a $1.60 old-fashioned chocolate donut that tasted remarkably like a sixty-cent old-fashioned chocolate donut. Across from me, drinking a mocha something-or-other, was an old friend. A very *trusted* old friend. Clarke McGuire was a defense attorney here in LA. Five years ago, Clarke hired me to help clear one of his clients of murder. The case started simple, but ended bad. Very bad. Someone had ended up dead, and Clarke and I had been at the wrong place at the wrong time, and suddenly we had a body to dump. And so we did, together, in the desert, in a grave we dug together. Call it a bonding experience. Now we shared a secret that we would take to our own graves, and since we were sharing secrets, I had let him in on a big one of my own.

Now Clarke McGuire, defense attorney, with his perfectly bald head and too big hands, was one of only three people on Earth who knew that Elvis Presley was living in obscurity in LA and working secretly as a private investigator.

Unless you counted the stalker.

Without looking up from his newspaper, Clarke said, "Happy birthday, by the way."

"Is that why you splurged for the donut?" I asked.

"That, and because you're broke again."

"Well, you're a day late," I said. "My birthday was yesterday."

"I'm a day late, and you're a dollar short."

"Oh, brother," I said.

Clarke chuckled to himself, turned the page, snapped the paper taut.

Starbucks was filled nearly to capacity. We sat alone in a corner, near the front entrance, at the only rectangular table the place offered, a table which was designated for the handicapped. I knew this because a little yellow wheelchair was routed into the wooden surface. I wasn't handicapped, and neither was Clarke. By all rights, this was an illegal coffee affair.

"We're sitting at the handicap table," I said.

"I know."

"Neither of us is handicapped," I said, "unless we count your baldness."

"Baldness isn't a handicap."

"Should be."

He shook his head. His *bald* head, that is. "I tried calling you yesterday," he said. "Your phone was off. Wanted to wish you a happy birthday."

"I hate my birthday."

"I know."

I was quiet. Clarke was reading the *LA Times*, or at least pretending to. More often than not, I caught him watching me. Clarke was a good friend, my only friend, but he was also infatuated with me. Sometimes I wished I had never divulged my secret to him. Surprise, it turned out he was quite the Elvis fan. Lucky me.

"She was on TV yesterday," I said. "Oprah."

Clarke nodded; he knew who *she* was. "How'd she look?"

"Beautiful," I said. "And sad. Always sad."

I was tracing the engraving of the wheelchair with my finger, listening to the chatter of orders at the nearby counter, everyone speaking a secret Starbucks language, meaningless to the uninitiated. I was suddenly wishing my drink had something stronger in it than just a shot or two of espresso.

"I'd do anything to see her again, Clarke."

"I know."

"Just one minute. One hug."

"Dead men don't give hugs."

"Thank you, Davy Jones."

He chuckled and turned back to his paper. We were silent some more. Starbucks was alive and well and running on caffeine. A few minutes later, without looking up, Clarke said, "I have a job for you if you're interested. Missing person case."

Working was good for me. It kept me sane. Kept my thoughts in check, my mind in check. It was damn easy for my life to spiral out of control if I let it. Working hard and helping others kept me grounded, alive. It also put food on my table.

"Tell me about it," I said.

"Missing female. Twenty-two, an actress. Missing now for three days."

"Haven't heard about it."

"And you won't. The mother wants to keep this quiet, if possible. Her daughter has a movie coming out this fall, and the mother doesn't want the bad publicity."

"Nice to see her priorities are in order."

Clarke shrugged. "Not my business," he said. "Ideally the girl is found safe and sound and the public is none the wiser."

"Except the public might have leads to her whereabouts."

"What can I say," he said. "I'm just their attorney."

"Fine," I said, "What does the LAPD have so far?"

"So far nothing, which is why the mother is hiring every available PI she can find."

"Even old ones?" I asked.

"Even old ones," said Clarke. "I told her that you're the best in the business at finding the missing, that, in fact, it's your specialty."

I finished the last of the donut. "Sometimes they're found dead, Clarke," I said.

"I know," he said. "I left that part out."

ACKNOWLEDGMENTS

Once again, my heartfelt thanks to Eve Paludan for her time and energy and friendship.

I am especially grateful to Sandra Hylton for her initial reading of the manuscript.

A special thank-you to Sandy for her generous help.

ABOUT THE AUTHOR

J.R. Rain is an ex–private investigator who now writes full-time in the Pacific Northwest. Chronically creative from an early age, he first fell in love with writing while making his very own Choose Your Own Adventure books as a child, and has since written thirty-three novels and three short-story collections, as well as screenplays for Paramount Pictures. Rain was born in Southern California and has lived up and down the West Coast. He currently resides just outside of Seattle, living in a small house on a small island with his small dog, Sadie, who has more energy than Robin Williams.

Made in the USA
Lexington, KY
11 October 2016